Brooke J. Losee

LOVE

&

MAGIC

Children of Magic: Book 2

Brooke J. Losee

LOVE

&

MAGIC

Children of Magic: Book 2

CHAPTER ONE
Meeting with the General

Strauth didn't typically find himself inside the elaborately decorated walls of the palace, but he couldn't ignore a summons from the general. His eyes wandered along the corridor, analyzing the details of the dark purple flags hanging every few feet. He traced the embroidered outline of the harpy eagle in the bottom corner of the banner closest to him. The creature, once idolized by his people as a savior of sorts, had failed them as of late.

At least, that was Strauth's opinion.

The bird had done nothing to save the army of Izarden from the workings of the dark sorcerer.

Strauth returned his focus to the door in front of him. At eye level, an intricately carved flower adorned the entry to the general's quarters. Every door along this wing of the palace—the area designated to those of the highest class and respected of King Delran—displayed finesse, and Strauth couldn't help but wonder what it was like to be held in such high esteem and be the recipient of the king's generosity.

His older brother, Ivrin, had earned it, of course. But not Strauth. Not yet.

Ivrin had taken their father's place after his death, and Strauth hoped to bring the old general honor, just as his brother had.

Strauth lifted his hands to the lapels of his black overcoat and adjusted the fabric to ensure he looked presentable. He drew in a deep breath and allowed his fist to make contact with the door. A few soft taps brought the sound of footsteps on the other side.

The door swung open, and Ivrin appeared in the frame. His black long-sleeved shirt matched Strauth's, but the piece also flaunted several dark purple embellishments and a few gold-trimmed pockets, indicators of the highest rank in the king's army.

At several inches taller than his brother, Strauth stared down at the man's stoic expression. Ivrin's blue eyes combed over him, and Strauth straightened under the scrutiny. Though his brother's build was much smaller than his own, Ivrin had a way of making anyone feel intimidated.

"Strauth, come in."

His tone was anything but welcoming, and certainly not one that suggested Ivrin had been the one to extend the invitation. This was the first time Strauth had visited his brother in his new home. In fact, it was the first time he'd set foot inside the palace at all. Despite having been the general, his father had chosen to live outside the fortified walls, insisting on a modest cottage for himself and his wife and two sons.

Ivrin had accepted the king's invitation to live in the palace straight away, leaving Strauth to occupy their old home alone.

Ivrin sat down behind his desk and stared at Strauth for a moment, scanning over his attire again. Strauth clasped his hands behind his back.

"You've done well," Ivrin said finally. "Not that I ever thought you wouldn't, of course. Runs in our blood, as Father always said. How long has it been now since you joined the army?"

"Since plague swept through Izarden." Strauth shifted under the weight of the sensitive topic, one he shouldn't have felt shy to discuss with his own family. "Since Mother passed."

"Ah, yes. I suppose that's right."

Strauth didn't know what more to say. He and Ivrin had never been close. Strauth could vaguely remember their interactions as children, and as adults, their relationship had been nearly nonexistent.

Silence stretched between them. Ivrin sighed. "Listen, I've never been good at this sort of thing. Relationships. Connections. It's just not in me to find happiness in rapport, but I can say our father would have been proud of how far you've come, and how quickly, for that matter."

"Thank you. That means a great deal to me."

Despite being family, Ivrin had paid Strauth little heed during his training. He supposed that displaying favoritism wasn't in a general's best interest, but that didn't mean Strauth didn't desire his brother's approval. This was the most he'd ever received.

Ivrin cleared his throat. "Right. Well, none of that is why I called you here. I've another matter to discuss."

Since Ivrin never offered anything that looked like a familial gesture, this could only be in regards to Strauth's position as a lieutenant. A new assignment, perhaps? To Strauth's knowledge, the king had no intention of continuing his father's efforts to seize the surrounding kingdoms—at least not yet. After the devastation caused by the sorcerer, Morzaun, there was much that needed to be taken care of in their own kingdom before calling the army to battle against another.

Ivrin held up a small piece of parchment. "I've received a letter."

Strauth's brows furrowed. A letter? From whom? And why would he need to discuss it with his younger brother? Unless it had come from family, of which they had none, Strauth could find little reason to be involved.

"I must ask that you keep the information I'm about to share with you to yourself. You are my confidant in this. Admittedly, I don't know you as well as I should, but as my only family, I am trusting you."

"You have my word, as both your brother and your lieutenant, that I will keep any information you share with me confidential unless otherwise instructed."

Ivrin's mouth curled a little, an almost smile. "Glad to hear it. This letter came from a man named Aldeth. Do you recognize the name?"

Strauth went rigid. "Yes, I do."

"I thought you might. In this letter, he has requested an audience with our king. He wishes to make amends."

"Amends?" Strauth asked, clenching his fists. "How does he expect to make amends?" He drew in a deep breath. This wasn't the time or place for anger.

Ivrin stood and moved to the front of his desk. He leaned against it, the small parchment waving in his hand. Strauth couldn't take his eyes off of it. The thought of who had written those words made his blood boil.

"Believe me, Strauth. I understand your resentment. It is for this reason that I have called you here tonight." Ivrin squared his shoulders. "I have responded to his request. I've made the petition to King Delran."

"You did what! Why?"

This time, when the corners of Ivrin's mouth moved, a full smile swept across his face—a malicious smile. "Because I can't kill him if I don't know where he is."

The reply took Strauth by surprise. Apparently, he and Ivrin had one thing in common—they both wanted Aldeth and all others who wielded magic dead.

Although Strauth had not been born when mercenaries had attacked Izarden nearly thirty years ago, his father had relayed the details to him many times in his youth. The invaders had destroyed countless villages, and laid siege on their great city. With the army decimated, Izarden had held little hope of survival until three children revealed their unnatural powers to Strauth's father. With their help, the mercenaries were defeated, and the kingdom was once again safe.

Or so they had believed.

The children were honored by the king, only to grow up and betray their kingdom. Morzaun and Aldeth sought power, and in their schemes to get it, many people had lost their lives, including Strauth's father.

Morzaun had continued his onslaught for years, leaving death and destruction in his wake. Though he'd been only a boy, Strauth could still remember the carnage and the terror his people had faced, knowing someone with magic could wipe them out at any moment. Hearing the anguished cries of those who'd lost loved ones to the sorcerer became a regular occurrence and left a dark shadow over his people. After a great battle between Morzaun and the army, one that resulted in King Sytal's death, Morzaun had simply disappeared.

Hundreds of lives lost, and the man hadn't paid for any of it.

"So, you plan to kill him?" asked Strauth. He needed the confirmation. For so long, he'd wanted nothing more than to eradicate magic and those who wielded it. They didn't belong among mankind. They were a threat to the entire land of Virgamor, and if someone didn't put an end to them now, there may not be anything left to save.

"Yes, I intend to kill them," said Ivrin. "All of them. Not just Aldeth. We must take care of his entire family if we are to eliminate this threat."

"I admit that I'm happy with your plan and desire the outcome more than anything, but do you think it wise to invite such a threat into our midst? And so near our king, no less?"

Ivrin folded his arms. "I will speak with the king about how close they will be permitted to come. I've requested for Aldeth to bring his whole family. Under the ruse of making amends, I'm hopeful the warlock will not realize our plan until it is too late. If we surprise them, we can take care of this problem with little resistance."

Strauth pursed his lips. His brother's plan seemed fairly sound, but they weren't dealing with normal people. Magic wasn't something to underestimate. "Are you certain the woman will not see the attack coming? Father said she possessed the ability to see the future."

"I've considered that," said Ivrin. "It's not something I can guarantee. Father often told me of their powers, so I'm aware of the extent of their magic. It will be a risk, but I see no other way to rid ourselves of this problem, and this may be our only opportunity to lure them out of hiding."

Facing someone with magic was complicated. There was no telling what dark spells those three children had learned over the years. Even if Ivrin had a small understanding of their powers, the three of them were each different in their own right.

"Aldeth's wife can see the future, and he can control the elements," said Strauth. "That combination alone is enough to give me pause. We have nothing that can defend against such things."

In years of drought and famine, Aldeth had offered his assistance to save the kingdom from starvation by restoring crops. But one good deed didn't excuse his evil ways. Because of magic, Strauth's father was dead, killed by the hands of the same man who had once saved Izarden.

Anger surged through him. Aldeth and Morzaun were proof of how much destruction could come from magic, and he refused to let them continue their paths of destruction. They would pay dearly for their crimes.

"And Morzaun?" Strauth asked. "How do you plan to take him on? No one has seen him since the great battle. I do not believe he will show himself as readily as Aldeth and his family."

"Agreed. Morzaun will be far more difficult to track down, but I am less concerned with him. According to Aldeth's letter, the man has been relieved of his magical power altogether. He poses far less of a threat right now."

"Relieved of his power? How is that possible?"

Ivrin shrugged. "Aldeth didn't give me the precise details, but from what I can conclude from his letter, it seems he and Yelene had a battle of their own with him. They claim to have used their magic to strip Morzaun of his. I must say, that piece of information brought me a small amount of happiness."

"A small amount," agreed Strauth. "But not enough to satisfy my desire for justice. And are you certain Morzaun is powerless? How do we know Aldeth even speaks the truth?"

"Our army has been searching for him for months, and he's made no more attempts to attack. I cannot say for certain, but my instincts tell me the man would not simply go into hiding if he still had the power to destroy us. Do not concern yourself with it. I assure you, Aldeth may have power, but he will not make any foolish attempts on the king's life."

Strauth didn't hold Ivrin's same confidence, but he could hardly argue when his brother's position demanded both respect and obedience. "Very well, but he deserves to pay for the crimes he committed. He deserves death for the blood on his hands. Nothing less."

Ivrin laid the letter on his desk and walked towards him. His hand met Strauth's shoulder. "Don't worry, my brother. We will get justice for our father. I will find Morzaun, but first we must make sure magic never harms another person in this kingdom—in Virgamor."

"We? Are you inviting me to take part in this plan?"

Ivrin's malicious grin returned. "I would think of doing nothing less, Strauth. You deserve justice as much as I do. We will do this together. We will do this for Father."

Strauth nodded, his chest swelling with unexpected warmth. Ivrin had never offered him so much attention. Perhaps working together would bring them closer. If Strauth could assist in his brother's plan, he might obtain both Ivrin's approval and justice for his father.

"How soon do we begin?"

CHAPTER TWO
Summons and Pardons

A calm breeze blew through the meadow, and a vast array of brightly colored flowers bent to its demands. The sun rested just above the mountain in the distance. Soon, the light would fade behind its majestic snow-capped peak. Feya drew in a breath of warm air, and the smell of the salty sea filled her nose.

She twirled a flower stem between her fingers, spinning the white petals until they blurred in a uniform circle. Feya plucked a few more from the ground, collecting them until she held a vibrant display. She imagined tossing them into the air and pushing them higher using her magic, only to allow them to fall like raindrops in a rainbow of color.

But the desire to follow through on the notion was fleeting.

She chucked the flowers to the ground, afraid the temptation would grow too strong to resist.

A few yards away, Ladisias whirled a sword through the air with grace and strength, while Zeeran practiced blocking his attacks. Feya knew little about sword fighting, but of her two brothers, Ladisias clearly had more skill and experience. She supposed his expertise came from the years of training he had received from their uncle—training Zeeran had only begun when...

She shook her head. She wouldn't allow her thoughts to linger on past events. Pushing them away was easier. Forgetting that aspect of her family's life and the fear that accompanied it was essential if she wanted to keep her anxiety at bay and move forward.

Zeeran swung his sword with so much effort that he nearly staggered to the ground when Ladisias dodged the attempt. Another swing landed him among the flowers. Ladisias heaved a sigh. "You can't attack in anger, Zeeran. It throws off your senses. You have to maintain focus at all times. Let your emotion flow with your attacks, not lead them."

Zeeran shifted on the grass, avoiding his mentor's gaze. His dipped chin caused the sunlight to catch on the short, dark whiskers of his upper lip and made Feya wonder if he intended to grow a beard like Ladisias. "Well, not all of us have such a natural aptitude for this, nor have I had a great instructor."

Ladisias frowned. "I'm sorry you find me unsatisfactory, but it isn't my fault that I'm your only option. Besides, you could be a great sword fighter if you would put your pride aside long enough to listen to me. Perhaps I'm not the best teacher, but that doesn't mean you can't learn. You have the skill; you simply lack the discipline to do anything with it."

"I have plenty of discipline, seeing as how I'm willing to put up with you and your unhelpful motivational speeches."

"Then prove it. You're not some spring sapling. Control your emotions."

Zeeran jumped to his feet with renewed determination. Her brothers had been rivals since they were young, and they often fought with each other. At twenty three—younger than Ladisias by three years—Zeeran had always followed in his brother's shadow. Feya suspected he found that frustrating at times.

For a moment, Zeeran clenched the hilt of his sword until his knuckles turned white, and then loosened his hold at the same time he exhaled, the tightness in his expression softening. "You're right. I'm sorry. I need to listen to you if I am to learn, but you make it rather difficult sometimes."

Ladisias lifted his sword, grinning. "Then let's continue, and I promise I'll try to be a better—more patient—mentor."

They continued for another hour until the sun had dipped behind the mountain peak and the clouds had turned bright orange and pink. Feya's eyes grew heavy as she watched them dance across the field of color from the shadows of an elm. Sweat dripped from their foreheads when they had finally finished for the day, and they collapsed in the shade next to her.

Ladisias lay flat on the ground and flashed her a crooked smile. "You look tired, Feya. Plucking flowers must be exhausting."

Feya narrowed her eyes. "What would you have me do? Join you? I can't see Papa being happy if his only daughter took to swinging a sword."

Ladisias propped himself up on his elbows, a piece of his light brown hair falling over his left eye and making him squint. "No, but what *would* make him happy is for his children to find their *happily ever afters*, but you don't seem inclined to do that either."

"Oh, just because I turned down one suitor—the only suitor on this blasted island—doesn't mean I'm against the idea of being courted. I'd just prefer someone who didn't treat me the same as the chickens he enjoys raising."

Ladisias grabbed his stomach, laughing. "Your blonde hair *does* remind me of his one bird. Clucky, I think it is?"

Feya whacked his shoulder several times, and he rolled away. "You're a horrible brother, do you know that?"

To her other side, Zeeran stared out over the meadow, seemingly lost to his own thoughts. He'd been so reserved the last few months, and after everything that had happened, Feya couldn't blame him. Uncertainty left a shadow hanging over them, like dark clouds looming just before a summer storm.

She touched his arm, and his dark brown eyes met hers. "Are you all right, Zeeran? You've been awfully quiet."

"I'm fine. Just thinking."

Growing up on an island where there were no other children meant her brothers had been her only companions. Feya had always been close to them. She'd often wondered what life away from the island was like. The only time she'd been beyond the shore was as an infant. She and her brothers had been young when her family sought refuge here. The treacherous waters surrounding the island kept visitors away, the perfect protection for those who needed to hide from the rest of Virgamor. Zeeran and Ladisias both claimed their memories of the time when they lived in Izarden had faded, but whether that was the truth or because they wanted to keep her spirit from longing to leave, she couldn't be sure.

Having been eight years old at the time, Ladisias likely remembered, but every time Feya clawed for details, he deflected. Either he wasn't fond of the memories, or he didn't want to give her ideas of grandeur. However, Feya didn't require her brother's memories for that. She wanted to leave, to experience the places beyond her tiny island world, even if only for a day.

Zeeran's voice pulled her from her thoughts. "I wonder what he's doing. Where he is?"

"Who?" she asked.

"Uncle Morzaun. Where do you suppose he's gone?"

"It's been five years. I don't know, nor do I want to know. Maybe it's good he's never come back."

"But he's our family? Don't you care that something could have happened to him? Especially now that he doesn't have magic?"

Truthfully, she didn't know how to answer that. She did care, but not to the extent Zeeran did. She suspected her brother missed their uncle, despite the things the man had done, but she couldn't bring herself to feel the same way. If Feya had ever possessed a connection with Morzaun, she had lost it the day he committed his horrendous acts against Izarden.

Ladisias rolled to his side to look at them. "Family or not, he's made his choices, and they haven't been good choices either." The stern look on his face reminded Feya of Papa. Of her two brothers, Ladisias resembled their father the most, with his golden brown hair and warm eyes. Zeeran, on the other hand, sported a head of black hair and possessed a slender build. "You shouldn't get angry about Uncle Morzaun's circumstances. He betrayed Izarden and left us all in a mess because of it. He only has himself to blame—"

Zeeran pushed himself from the ground with a scowl. "You know that isn't true. Uncle Morzaun would have never done those things if it wasn't for Sytal. He's the traitor. Why shouldn't I be angry about that? Why aren't *you* angry about it? You were closer to him than any of us."

Ladisias sat up and drew a deep breath. "Sytal was a traitor, but it still doesn't excuse the things our uncle has done. We have to move on, Zeeran. We have to let it go."

Zeeran's expression fell, lines of sadness burrowing into his forehead. "I suppose you're right, Ladisias, but I don't know how to move on. It feels as though our lives have been stolen from us and all we can do is hide." Zeeran sat back down on the grass and picked at the blades. "Do you think we'll ever be able to leave the island? Live somewhere besides here? I know the people of Izarden hate magic, but do you think *they* will ever move on?"

Feya understood how he felt. She'd often wondered the same thing. Verascene was a beautiful place to live, but it was also confining. There was more to life than the simple one here, secluded from the rest of the world. Perhaps if she could leave, she would actually find someone worth courting. Perhaps her heart could find its place.

"I don't know," said Ladisias. "I'd like to think that people could see us for who we are—could see magic for the good it can do—but I fear many minds have been tainted. It will take a great deal of work to change them, but I believe it's worth the effort."

And that effort would come from them alone. Feya's family was the only ones in all of Virgamor capable of using magic, a gift bestowed to her parents and uncle when they were her age and passed on to their children. They had desired a way to help the people of Izarden, and fate had provided them with powerful abilities to do so, but in the end, those same abilities had only left them in a mess of trouble.

Ladisias rose to his feet and offered Feya his hand with a smile. "Come on. Let's go see about dinner. I'm sure Mama and Papa are waiting for us."

Feya accepted, and he pulled her from the ground. Ladisias had always enjoyed teasing her, but he could be a gentleman when he wanted. He still found moments to taunt or badger her until her cheeks burned, but those moments had become less frequent as they'd grown older. Part of her missed his pestering. She should leave such childish notions behind, but the thought of growing up and losing any connection with the few people she knew made her heart ache.

They crossed the meadow and followed the dirt path through the village until they reached the stone cottage at the end. A lantern hung just inside the window, and Papa's shadowy figure moved across the room. He greeted them when they entered and gestured for them to join Mama at the table near the back wall.

"The three of you were out late," said Papa, sitting down and scooping some food onto his plate. "What have you been up to today?" He smiled, but there was something more behind his eyes. Feya could see it—a hint of restlessness.

Ladisias stuck a sizable chunk of potato into his mouth and swallowed before answering. "I've been training Zeeran. He's catching on." He passed his brother a wink, and Zeeran's lips lifted. "We'll have another expert swordsman in the family in no time. And Feya exhausted herself pruning the meadow."

Feya wrinkled her nose and scowled at him.

Papa stared at his plate, nodding, oblivious to Ladisias's nettlesome comments. "Good. That's very good."

Feya's eyes darted from Papa to Mama, who appeared just as anxious. They were hiding something, but what? Verascene wasn't an eventful place. She'd learned that in her eighteen years of life here. The place was home to less than three dozen people. So, to see both her parents in such a state had her concerned. It wasn't like either of them to act so withdrawn.

Papa cleared his throat. "You may need to put off training for a bit, Zeeran."

Her brother narrowed his eyes. "Why?"

Ladisias had stopped eating and was now watching Papa carefully. The silence seemed to drag on. Papa sighed. "I've been in contact with the general of Izarden."

Zeeran's eyes widened. "What? Why would you contact him? If we're not careful, they could find us!"

Papa raised his hand and gave him a look that said *calm down*. "I know that, Zeeran. I assure you—I've been careful. My purpose in sending him a letter was to request an audience with the king."

Ladisias twisted a strand of his hair around his finger. "Why would you want to meet with King Delran? Surely he would not accept an offer after all that's happened? The people of Izarden are terrified of magic because of what Morzaun did."

"I know how it sounds, but I thought if he would entertain a meeting with me, I could sort out this mess your uncle has created. I dislike being the focus of so much disdain. For the sake of our future, I feel it pertinent to request a pardon from King Delran, explain to him that my family was not involved in the incident against his father."

Zeeran pounded his fist on the table. "A pardon? Why should we need a pardon if we have done nothing wrong! King Sytal got what he deserved. The people of Izarden should thank Morzaun for what he did. Sytal was an evil man, and—"

"Zeeran, please!" Mama touched his arm. "I know this is hard, but there's no excuse for your uncle's actions, justified or not. We have an opportunity to make peace with it all. I don't want this to hang over my family—my children...grandchildren."

Feya and her brothers squirmed. None of them were ready for that phase of their lives. And how could they be when they were trapped on an island? The only people who lived there besides her family did so because they had become stranded at one point or another. Shipwrecked or marooned—the few who survived the perilous sea became trapped, just as they were, leaving Feya and her siblings no options in regards to settling down like their parents had. Perhaps Papa was right. Maybe a pardon would give them the freedom to leave Verascene and start a new life.

But freedom to leave and the ability to live without judgment were two very different things. Feya wondered if the last was achievable at all.

Papa folded his arms and sighed. "I wrote to General Ivrin hoping he would help us gain an audience with Delran. If nothing else, the people of Izarden deserve to know the truth about what happened. The general has responded to my letter, and King Delran has agreed to the meeting. I think it's in our best interest to go...to try to make this right."

Feya's heart lurched. "*Our*?" She shouldn't allow herself to hope for such a thing. Papa likely meant he and Mama were to go alone. But maybe...

"Yes, the king has asked for us all to come."

The chair screeched against the floor as Zeeran pushed it away from the table and stood. "You are being foolish! How can we trust such a request? How do we know they won't kill us the minute we enter the palace?"

"I don't intend to take you and Feya into the palace. You will come with us but are to remain outside the gate, hidden, until we return.

Ladisias has enough skill with his magic and sword that I needn't worry about him. Not that I don't think you do, Zeeran"—Papa's gaze drifted to Feya—"but I think it best you stay with your sister. I trust you to keep her safe. I want us to do this together. We are all each other has, and the world will always view us differently, no matter the outcome of this journey."

Zeeran scoffed. "Differently. Yes, Papa, the world will always fear magic and those who wield it. Is that not what got us into this predicament in the first place? Sytal feared magic would be used against him. What makes you think his son will be any different?"

For the first time, Papa gave him a glare that burned with warning. Papa was the most docile and patient person Feya knew, always slow to anger and someone who preferred to avoid conflict whenever possible—a stark contrast to Zeeran's fiery temperament.

"Sytal's father was a man of honor—a man who fought for peace," said Papa. "One cannot judge another solely on their family. Judgment should come from a person's deeds, not their lineage."

"You would put us all in danger in hopes that this man is nothing like his father? You would put your children's lives at risk? What does that say about *your* deeds?"

Papa rose, his eyes narrowed and his fists clenched. Mama placed her hand on his arm. "Please, we must stay calm. Fighting among ourselves will do us no favors. Of course, we don't want to put you in danger, but your father and I fear that doing nothing will put a target on our family in perpetuity. We will take every precaution we can when we visit Izarden. Don't forget. We still have magic on our side."

Zeeran ran his hands through his hair and heaved a sigh. "Magic or not, this is dangerous, and in my opinion, a pointless risk. Why put our lives on the line for something that won't even help the situation?"

"A pardon *will* help," said Papa. "I'm sure of it. Your mother is right. We don't want to be the targets of the king's wrath forever. Our family deserves better than that. *You* deserve a better life than that."

"Perhaps if you hadn't spared the life of a traitor, we *would* have a better life!" Zeeran slapped the cup sitting on the table, spilling water across the surface. The piece rolled and clattered against the floor. "This is a fool's errand!" He stormed from the cottage into the darkness.

Mama sniffled and waved her hands, a bright purple light encompassing them. The cup floated from the floor, and she guided it to the table. Papa followed suit, waving his hands until his own green aura appeared. With his movements, droplets of water gathered in the air, sparkling with the reflection of the lantern light, and moved back into the cup.

Magic could be a beautiful thing.

Ladisias drummed his fingers against the table and stood. "I'll go talk to Zeeran. Calm him down." He paused in the doorframe, his expression solemn. "When should we expect to leave?"

"At first light," said Papa. "This is not a journey to delay."

CHAPTER THREE
Dark Schemes

Strauth passed through the front gate. Sunlight glistened off the white marble walls of the palace, and warm rays made his skin bead with sweat beneath his black military uniform. He wiped his forehead and nodded to one of the guards, whose dark attire matched his own, when they opened the door for him.

Ivrin had requested Strauth meet him this morning, and he hoped their discussion would be in regards to the plan they had contrived a week ago. He was eager to set things into motion. The sooner magic was eliminated, the better.

His brother stood in the foyer with his hands clasped behind his back, staring out the paned window into the courtyard. His dirty blond hair covered his ears, slight curls resting on the back of his neck—the same way Strauth's did. The two of them had always looked quite similar, minus their difference in height, but at eight years more than Strauth's five and twenty, Ivrin's hair contained a few strands of silver.

Strauth stopped a few feet behind Irvin and cleared his throat. "Good morning, General."

Ivrin spun around. "Ah. Good morning, Lieutenant. I'm glad you're here."

Strauth's heart pounded. Perhaps today would be the day they received justice. The man responsible for their father's death had walked free for far too long. "Have you received a reply from Aldeth?"

Ivrin smiled. "I have. In fact, he is due to arrive shortly. I wanted you to be here."

"What's the plan? Are you truly going to allow him near the king?"

The general placed his hand on Strauth's shoulder and gave it a firm squeeze. "Come. Everything will be explained to you. King Delran awaits us in the Great Hall."

He gestured for Strauth to follow him down a long corridor with rows of flags on one side and intricately framed windows on the other. They passed through a grand arch, entering the throne room, and Strauth took in the details of the elaborate paintings and hanging banners of dark purple. King Delran sat on a throne near the back wall, a statue of a black harpy eagle behind him. Its wings curled around the chair, as if to protect it and the person who sat upon the golden chair. At one time, the image would have proved true, but magic had changed that. Waiting for the legendary bird to save Izarden would only result in the kingdom's destruction. They needed to take matters into their own hands.

Ivrin and Strauth stopped in front of the king and both bent into low bows. "General Ivrin," said Delran with a nod. "And I assume this is your brother, Lieutenant Strauth?"

"Yes, Your Highness."

Delran's gaze floated over Strauth from head to foot. The constant scrutiny made him uncomfortable, but what could he do about it? "Have you informed him of our plan?" asked the king.

Ivrin clasped his hands behind his back. "Not yet, My King. I thought I'd allow you the honor. I assure you we can trust my brother; he is eager to participate."

Delran's black mustache twitched as he looked Strauth over again. "Very well. Aldeth and his family have arrived and are waiting to be escorted inside. I intend to offer him a pardon."

"What?"

The word escaped before Strauth could stop himself. He pinched his lips to keep anything more from spilling out. Now wasn't a good time to forget where he stood or who sat before him.

Fortunately, Delran seemed amused by his outburst, a slight smile curling on his lips. "In exchange for this pardon, he will provide a service to Izarden. We need to find the dark sorcerer, Morzaun, and our best chance of achieving this is with his help. Morzaun has evaded me for far too long, and it's time he paid for his crimes."

Strauth shifted, wringing his hands together. "And if he brings you Morzaun, you will offer him a pardon?"

"Yes. He and his family."

Strauth hadn't been expecting this. While the king's proposal held merit and would draw out the man responsible for his father's death, he couldn't help but be disappointed. He didn't just want justice. He wanted magic eradicated.

"Forgive me, My King, but do you think granting Aldeth's request is wise? His magic still poses a threat to our people. What if he—"

"I think my plan is the key to getting what I want—Morzaun's head on a silver platter. Catching him is my priority. The man killed my father, the ruler of our great kingdom, and he deserves a traitor's death." Strauth's shoulders slumped, but the king continued, "However, should something happen to these magic wielders—should an accident befall them after the traitor is brought to me—I would not feel any need to seek justice, nor do I believe the people would demand it."

Strauth's spirits lifted. The king passed him a knowing look and Strauth nodded. Delran was not against the scheme to rid the world of magic, but it would need to be conducted in the shadows.

"I understand, Your Highness," said Strauth.

"Good. Now that we have an understanding, we can bring them in." Delran clapped, and a guard disappeared through the archway into the corridor. Strauth held his breath. Seconds later, the guard returned with two men and a woman, ushering them before the king who fixed them with stern eyes.

All three of them offered their respects with low bows and a curtsy. At least they had the sense to honor the king.

"Thank you for obliging my request, Your Highness," said the one man, whom Strauth decided must be Aldeth, judging by the wrinkle of skin below his eyes. The second was nearer to his own age and far too young to be the warlock his father had often spoken of.

"I admit it came as a surprise. After everything Morzaun has done, I'm afraid those who wield magic have lost the trust of the people of Izarden. It's been years, Aldeth. What made you decide to come out of hiding?"

"I understand, Your Highness. What I want more than anything is for those affected to have justice and for the truth to be known. My family and I have no desire to harm anyone. We only want peace and to earn back the trust of the people."

King Delran rose from his throne and stepped down from the dais to them. "You say you want our trust, and yet you have come here without your family, as I requested. I know you have more than one child, Aldeth. At least two more. Where are they?"

Aldeth stiffened, and the man next to him clenched his jaw. "My family has accompanied me, but I didn't—"

"Trust us enough to bring them to the palace? Seems hypocritical and not the best way to earn *my* trust." Delran lifted a brow, and Aldeth squirmed.

Looking over Aldeth for the first time, Strauth took in his sleek trousers and finely crafted overcoat. He'd parted his golden brown hair to one side, and the younger man, presumably his son, matched him in every manner. The woman, Yelene, stood silently in her flowy pale yellow gown. She could have passed for a genteel lady had this meeting been a grand ball instead. Strauth had expected something different from the people that stood before them. Aldeth presented himself as more like a gentleman than a dark warlock. But then again, acts were meant to deceive.

Aldeth hung his head. "You are right, My King. Please forgive me. My youngest son and daughter are currently waiting outside the palace gate."

"Fetch them."

Aldeth's brows furrowed. "My King? Is that truly necess—?"

Delran held up his hand to silence him and then pointed to the other man. "You. What is your name?"

"Ladisias," he answered.

"Ladisias will retrieve the rest of your family, and once he has returned, we will discuss the terms of your pardon."

Aldeth shook his head. "Your Highness, I—"

"Enough! Your family will not be harmed today, so long as you keep your power in check. Go get them."

Aldeth opened his mouth to rebuff, but quickly snapped it closed.

"Father?" Ladisias whispered, deep concern etched into his features.

"It's all right, Ladisias. Please do as the king has asked and get your brother and sister." Ladisias cocked his head to one side and gave Aldeth a look that suggested he disagreed with the arrangement. "Please, Ladisias."

Ladisias's eyes met Strauth's. Distrust filled their depths. Strauth supposed he couldn't blame the man for being cautious. Both parties were on edge, but if the magic wielders wanted their pardon, they would have to play Delran's game.

With a heavy sigh, Ladisias left the Great Hall. Silence reigned, and minutes felt like hours to Strauth. Yelene shifted closer to her husband and lifted on her toes to whisper in his ear.

"Something you'd like to share?" asked Delran.

Aldeth wrapped his fingers around her hand, and she buried her face in his shoulder. "She's just afraid, as any parent might be in this situation."

Afraid? Strauth mulled over the notion. Magic didn't make these people invincible, but it certainly granted them an unprecedented advantage. That Yelene feared *them*, people who stood little chance against their power, baffled him.

"So long as you pose no threat, you have no reason to fear." Delran's gaze flicked to Strauth and Ivrin.

"My family has done nothing to harm the people of Izarden," said Aldeth. "We do not condone Morzaun's actions, which is why Yelene and I took it upon ourselves to put an end to his path of destruction."

King Delran gestured to Ivrin and Strauth. "Tell that to my general and lieutenant. You were there the day their father was murdered in cold blood in this very hall. So do not patronize us."

Aldeth's face paled, and his eyes darted between them. "General Fyord was your father? Yes, I suppose I can see the resemblance. I am so sorry for your—"

"Don't!" Strauth spat. "We don't want your sympathy. If it's trust you hope to earn, then I'm afraid you will only be disappointed. I will never trust magic or anyone who uses it."

Delran chuckled, which irked Strauth, but his emotions were so volatile he figured that was the reason. "You see, Aldeth," said

Delran, folding his arms. "Morzaun's actions have tainted any good that ever came from magic. I recognize that you have helped us in the past, but I cannot change the minds of my people. That will require work on your part."

Aldeth nodded. "Of course, My King. If we can use our magic to help our people, then we would be happy to do so."

They would help all right. Aldeth would assist in the capture of a dark sorcerer. Justice would be served. And then, when they least expected it, when they believed they had earned a pardon for their misdeeds, their lives would end. Virgamor would be safe from the workings of magic, once and for all.

CHAPTER FOUR
A Fear of Magic

Green eyes peered at her from the shadows, catching the flicker of lantern light from across the room. The hair on Feya's arms stood on end, and she froze under the predatory gaze, barely able to make out the human silhouette. The glint of a jagged blade reflected on the white marble wall. The figure rushed from the darkness towards her with a dagger poised at shoulder height.

She gasped, her eyes snapping open, and a hand touched her shoulder. Zeeran looked her over with pinched brows. "You all right?"

Feya nodded. "Just a silly dream."

Zeeran dropped his gaze and fidgeted with the buttons on his coat. In an effort to calm her nerves, Feya had dozed off, but the short nap hadn't done her any good—not when a shadowy figure was trying to kill her. Thank goodness the images hadn't been real.

Feya pressed her back against the wall of the barn and rolled a piece of straw between her fingers. Wafts of hot, malodorous air met her nose every time a horse moved about in their stall, making her face wrinkle. There were half a dozen in the stuffy wooden structure, most of them quiet and unmoving in the heat of a hot summer day. The longer she and Zeeran sat in the shadows, the more she longed to greet the fresh air and enjoy the afternoon.

The last few days had been exceptionally tiresome, partially because of their long journey to get here and partially because of her mounting excitement. Leaving Verascene had been nothing short of thrilling. She'd enjoyed every moment aboard their ship as it drifted across the sea. With his magic, Papa had guided the vessel safely away from the treacherous waves that surrounded the island. The gentle rocking across the glistening water had calmed her soul in a way she hadn't expected.

Zeeran hadn't experienced the same pleasant sensation. The motion had made him sick, and he had spent much of their sea voyage bent over the ship's railing. Feya felt sorry for her brother, but he seemed better now that his feet rested firmly on dry land.

Once they arrived in Rowenport, Papa had purchased horses to make the last leg of their trip to Izarden, which she'd only partially utilized after getting sore the first day. She wasn't used to riding in a saddle, nor on a horse. Verascene hosted its share of animals, but they were a bit different, to say the least. Feya had chosen to walk the second day. Her family had camped the previous night along the dirt road to the kingdom's great city and arrived just before noon this morning. Papa had petitioned an old friend for the temporary use of his barn. The old man had agreed to allow Feya and Zeeran to hide there until their family returned from their meeting with the king. Zeeran had been reluctant to trust the man at first, but Feya had felt no hesitation. His soft amber eyes and warm smile had earned her confidence immediately.

She just wished they didn't have to hide out in the barn all day. How long would this meeting take, anyway? Their hiding place was only a few minutes' walk from the palace gate, but Mama, Papa, and Ladisias had been gone for over an hour already. Would the king grant their request? Offer them a pardon? She hoped he would. Perhaps such a thing would be the start of a new life for her and her family. Perhaps they could return to Izarden. The short time she'd spent here had only increased her desire for something more than life on the island, where she often felt alone. Here, she had the potential to make friends her age; at least she held hope that she might.

But that was all under the assumption that Papa found success in his endeavors with the king. She shuddered to think what would happen should the man deny their request. The people of Izarden didn't trust magic, and coming here had been risky.

She shifted on the pile of straw beneath her and sighed. Zeeran, who was sitting beside her with his legs sprawled out and his head leaning against the wall, turned to face her. "Are you sure you're all right?”

“Fine. Just anxious, I suppose. I’m ready to get out of this smelly barn.”

Zeeran chuckled, and the sound warmed her soul. Her brother rarely laughed these days, and hearing even a small expression of amusement from him made her happy. He picked up a handful of straw and tossed it in front of him. “It is rather smelly, isn’t it? Almost as unbearable as Ladisias’s shoes.”

Feya snorted. “Almost. I used to put flowers in them, thinking it would somehow erase the odor, but the mixture only made things worse.”

A full burst of laughter escaped him. “I recall him complaining about that. He’d stick his feet in and find a bunch of squishy petals. I believe he still checks before putting them on, even now. Ladisias always thought you did it as an act of revenge for his teasing.”

“No, I simply wanted to save us all from misery. Shame it didn’t work.”

Zeeran placed his arm around her and flashed her a smile. “If nothing else, you provided me with bounds of entertainment.”

“Glad I could help.”

Feya leaned into him, resting her head on his shoulder. At least she didn’t have to wait here alone. Zeeran was the perfect distraction to keep her mind from combing over all the scenarios of how the day could go, most of which were unpleasant.

“How do you think it’s going?” she whispered.

“I don’t know. I’m not sure if them being gone so long is a good thing or a bad thing.”

Her stomach twisted. What would they do if Mama, Papa, and Ladisias didn't return? What if the king detained them instead of granting the pardon? How would she and her brother even know? The thoughts tore at her insides. Waiting to find out was the worst form of torture.

"Everything will be fine," said Zeeran, placing his chin on top of her head. "Don't think about it. Just talk to me instead."

"What should we talk about?"

He made a humming sound, and Feya could feel the vibration rumbling from his chest. "Perhaps we should think of a way to pester Ladisias while he isn't around to interrupt or catch us."

Feya giggled. "What did you have in mind?"

"Well, you could put him to sleep, and I—"

"No." She straightened to look into his dark eyes. "Nothing that involves magic."

Zeeran's forehead furrowed. "A sleeping spell won't hurt him, Feya." She shook her head, and Zeeran heaved a heavy sigh. "It's been a long time since I've seen you use your magic. Why do you hold yourself back?"

Her brother was right. She hadn't used her magic in a long time, nearly a year, to be exact. The restraint had started with slow doubts after the events involving her uncle and had slowly filled her with enough fear that she dared not use her power at all. The less she allowed her purple aura to manifest itself, the more difficult it had become to summon it. Last time she tried, she'd produced nothing for her effort. Perhaps suppressing her magic had eliminated it entirely.

"I don't think I can anymore," she whispered. The admission both soothed and scared her. Without magic, she felt vulnerable. Having a hidden weapon had always made her feel safer, yet at the same time, she feared what magic was capable of. Uncle Morzaun had displayed just how destructive it could be, and the last thing Feya wanted was to be like him—to hurt people.

"Sure you can," said Zeeran. He held his hand out, palm up, in front of them. "Just follow my lead."

The words to their strange language flowed from his lips, and a blue flame appeared above his hand. Zeeran's magic wasn't the same as Mama's or Papa's. He was a Protesta, just like their uncle. Ladisias's aura was green, signifying that he was an Elementalist. Like Papa, he had control over the elements and nature. Mama often had visions of the future, and her aura manifested as a glittering purple. Feya's was the same, or at least it had been. She'd never experienced visions, and now she wondered if she ever would.

An orb of blue light illuminated the barn. "Now you try," said Zeeran. "I know you can use the *illustris*. I've seen you do it before."

Feya nibbled at her lip. Did she dare unleash her power? The flow of magic through her body had brought her comfort as a child, but now the thought of using it only filled her with unease. Still, being in their current situation, knowing whether her abilities remained accessible might prove important.

She held out her hand the same way Zeeran had and let the words roll from her tongue. Though she hadn't uttered the foreign phrases in months, they came to her like a lost memory ready to resurface. Feya focused on her hand, waiting for the purple glow to encompass it.

But it never came.

After several moments without success, she dropped her hand back into her lap. Perhaps her power really was gone.

Zeeran squeezed her shoulder. "You just need to start practicing again. I'm sure it will come back to you with time. Hiding your magic away won't help, though. It's like a muscle; the more you use it, the stronger it becomes."

And therein lay her problem. Feya wasn't certain she wanted her powers to grow stronger. She feared what she and her magic could do. What if she couldn't control it? What if she became like their uncle?

Shivers spread over her skin. "I don't know, Zeeran. I'm not certain I *want* it back."

Her brother opened his mouth to respond, but the door to the barn swung open. Both of them stiffened as a shadowed figure entered. The light trickling down from the loft illuminated Ladisias's features as he stepped forward, but the realization of who the figure was did nothing to ease Feya's pounding heart. Deep lines filled his expression, and all the horrendous scenarios Feya had imagined for the past hour flooded her thoughts.

Zeeran lifted from the straw and brushed his trousers free of the scratchy pieces. "Where are Mama and Papa?"

Ladisias's gaze dropped to the floor, and Feya's heart lurched into her throat. Had something happened to them? How had Ladisias gotten away? More horrific images plagued her thoughts.

"They're still at the palace," her older brother said, meeting her gaze. He took in her expression. "And they're fine."

Her shoulders slumped. That was good news, but why had Ladisias returned without them?

"King Delran wasn't happy when we showed up without the two of you. He knew there were three of us and said Papa had not held up his end of the request. The king sent me to bring you back. Said we would discuss the terms of our pardon once I had returned."

"No way!" Zeeran shoved past him and began pacing along the stalls. Several horses whinnied at his aggressive march. "What if he's luring us into a trap? How can we expose ourselves like this?"

Ladisias shook his head. "Whether it is or isn't, it's too late now. If we don't go back, they'll surely mark Mama and Papa as a threat. Who knows what will happen. Our best chance is to play along with Delran's game, at least for now. I won't abandon our parents."

Zeeran rubbed his hands over his face. "I told him this was a foolish thing to do. We never should have left Verascene."

Feya slipped past Ladisias and placed her hand on Zeeran's arm. "Maybe you're right, but we can't leave Mama and Papa. We have to go. I don't want to put them in danger. This could still all work itself out."

His brows furrowed. Her brother likely didn't believe those words—she wasn't even sure if she believed them—but she wouldn't risk her family's life. If going to the palace gave them a chance at a pardon, a chance to put the past behind them, then she would take that risk.

"Please, Zeeran. I'm scared. Come with me."

Zeeran's face softened, and he slid his hand around hers. "All right." He turned to face Ladisias. "Anything we should know before we do this?"

"We'll be meeting with the king in the Great Hall, in addition to the general and one of his lieutenants."

"I don't like this," said Zeeran. "But you're right. If we don't go, they'll grow suspicious of Mama and Papa. There's no telling what Delran might do to them. We'd better get going before you're gone too long."

Zeeran started to pull his hand away from Feya, but she clasped it tightly. He offered her a small smile, and with a heavy heart, she followed his gentle guidance out of the barn.

CHAPTER FIVE
New Assignments

Footsteps echoed in the corridor, causing Strauth's heart rate to increase. More magic wielders. Aldeth's entire family. They would all be in one room, and he would commit their every detail to his memory. He would now know what his targets all looked like, and soon, he and his brother would see to it they were eliminated.

Ladisias entered first, the spitting image of his father—golden blond hair and a tall, thick build. Even without magic, the man could likely hold his own in a fight. He might prove difficult to subdue and require a more thoughtful strategy. A second man entered, one who looked nothing like his father or brother. Waves of dark hair fell over his ears and into his eyes, and his slender body looked half the size of his brother's.

Following behind him was Aldeth's youngest. Golden hair fell over her shoulders, flowing all the way down to her waist. Her dark purple dress matched the hanging banners of the Great Hall, but the petite figure the fabric concealed kept his interest far more than the embroidered designs of the harpy eagle stitched on their kingdom's crest. The woman possessed an uncommon beauty, one that, had she been a lady of nobility, would have had many men fighting for an ounce of her attention.

Yet her expression matched none of that. Fear was engraved into every part of her face. She kept close to her dark-haired brother, nearly on his heels as they neared them, and when they stopped beside their mother and father, she tucked herself behind Aldeth.

"My King, allow me to introduce my other son, Zeeran." Aldeth gestured to the man with black hair and then to the woman partially hidden behind him. "And this is my daughter, Feya."

Her eyes finally lifted from the floor, revealing a dark blue gaze that reminded Strauth of the sea, a color more rich than his own blue-grey. For the briefest moment, they met his before falling back to the floor.

"Very well," said King Delran. "Now that we are *all* here—" he lifted a brow and gave Aldeth a chiding look—"we can discuss the terms of your requested pardon. I'm inclined to grant it, but I will require something of you in exchange."

Zeeran scoffed, and his father glared at him. It seemed the young man found little surprise in the king's statement. But what had he expected? To just be given amnesty without any effort on their part? Magic had done too much damage for that. Surely, these magic wielders weren't that naïve?

"How can my family be of service to you, My King?" asked Aldeth, his voice low and tone humble. An act, no doubt.

"As you are aware, a certain sorcerer has committed horrific acts against the kingdom of Izarden and, more particularly, against my family. It is my deepest desire that this man receives punishment. I've spent years chasing after him, and he remains elusive to my efforts. I need help finding him. Your powers will prove useful in my efforts to detain this criminal and bring justice to those affected by his acts of treason."

Aldeth shifted, and his throat bobbed with a hard swallow. "May I ask what you intend to do with Morzaun once he is captured, Your Highness? I wish to see my wife's brother pay for his crimes, but I will not play the role of executioner."

Delran picked at some lint on his coat, seemingly unconcerned by the question, and flicked it onto the floor. "I'm not asking you to kill him. I realize he is still your family; however, he deserves to stand trial for what he has done. The people will decide his fate, per our law. I cannot promise you they will be lenient with his crimes."

Aldeth and his wife exchanged looks, and the warlock sighed. "I cannot ask any more. Morzaun is overdue to pay the consequences of his actions, though it is hard for me to wish death upon him. As you so aptly put it, he is still family." He gave one last look to Yelene, and she nodded. "We will assist you in finding him, so that a trial might serve justice."

"What?" Zeeran rushed to his father's side, his face red. "We can't do this! I won't betray Uncle Morzaun. Please tell me you aren't cons—"

"Quiet, Zeeran." Aldeth's eyes burned with warning.

Zeeran shrank to his mother's side, deep lines chiseled into his forehead.

"Forgive us, My King," said Aldeth, returning his attention to Delran. His expression remained composed, but his family failed to hide their own concern and disdain. Yelene held Zeeran's shoulders and whispered something into his ear, but it was Feya's petrified gaze that captured Strauth. Even from his distance several yards away, he could see how her hand trembled at her side. How these people, who held so much power at their fingertips, could quake in such fear before them, he still couldn't comprehend, and the young woman seemed to harbor it more than the others.

Her eyes lifted and caught his stare. Strauth quickly averted his gaze.

"If you help us capture Morzaun, I will grant you and your family the pardon you desire as a token of gratitude for your services." Delran stroked his long black beard. "My general and a few of our most trusted men will accompany you, of course."

Aldeth nodded. "I accept your offer. We will do our part to help Izarden find peace."

"I've no doubt you will. As you've already forgone part of my request once today, I'll need some reassurance. I'd like to trust that you won't betray your king or Izarden, but as I've said before, the destruction caused by magic has tainted my ability to offer confidence without cause."

Aldeth clenched his jaw. "What kind of reassurance?"

"You, your wife, and your sons will assist General Ivrin in our search for Morzaun. The girl will stay here until you have found success."

The warlock's face paled. "You wish my daughter to stay at the palace while we search? My King, she can help us in our—"

"She stays. A good motivation for you to return and to not cross me, I should think."

Feya clutched her father's arm, her eyes wide.

"I assure you the motivation is unnecessary. I give you my word."

Delran scoffed. "Your word means nothing to me at the moment, Aldeth. The girl stays. She will be well tended in your absence. Bring me Morzaun, and your family leaves with a pardon. It's a simple arrangement, but one I will not offer you again."

Aldeth's fingers drummed against his thigh. "You swear no harm will befall her while she is here?"

With the perfect expression of nonchalance, Delran answered, "You have my honor that no harm will befall her by my order."

Clever. Delran had all but given Strauth and Ivrin permission to proceed, but the approval couldn't be classified as an order. He had to give the king due credit for his wise wording. But would Aldeth accept the terms?

Yelene grabbed Aldeth's arm, her voice a quiet whisper. "We can't just leave her here."

"We don't have a choice if we want to end this shadow hanging over us. Without the pardon, our family will never be free of it."

Delran tapped his foot. "I require an answer."

Yelene's shoulders slumped. "If you believe it is the only way. I have seen nothing to suggest she won't be safe, but..." The woman glanced at her daughter and sighed. "I suppose if she must."

"All right," said Aldeth, visibly unsettled. "Feya will remain here, per your request."

Zeeran started towards his father, but his mother gripped his shoulders and held him in place. She whispered in his ear again, and his body relaxed, but the flames in his eyes never subsided.

"Papa?" Feya's whisper hung in the air with a desperate plea.

Aldeth pulled her against him and enfolded her in his arms. "Everything is going to be all right. I promise." He leaned closer, whispering something Strauth couldn't hear, and Feya nodded.

Delran turned to Strauth with a pleased smile. "Lieutenant, please escort Miss Feya to a guest room"—he tossed a metal ring with a single key to him—"and see to it she is comfortable."

"Past the foyer and to the right," Ivrin muttered from beside him.

Why Delran couldn't ask one of the guards standing by the archway, he didn't know, but Strauth dipped into a bow and moved to follow his king's command. Feya tucked closer to Aldeth, watching his approach with terror.

"Come with me," he ordered, stopping just in front of them.

Aldeth squeezed her one last time before pulling her away. "Go with him. We will be back as soon as we can. I promise."

She turned to face Strauth, but froze under his gaze, her feet not moving more than an inch. He had no patience for this. Strauth curled his hand around her upper arm and tugged her forward. Her only rebuff was a sharp gasp as he guided her across the room.

"Hey!" Zeeran's shout echoed behind them. "Take it easy with my sister!"

Taps against the floor followed them, but only for a moment, replaced by Aldeth's reprimand. "Zeeran, stay calm! Everything is going to be fine!"

Whatever words followed were too muffled for him to understand. When Strauth reached the entry into the corridor, Feya resisted, briefly, looking over her shoulder at her family.

"Keep moving," said Strauth, bringing her even with him.

She said nothing during their walk down the long corridor to the guest wing. Strauth threw open the door to the first room and placed her inside. See to it that she was comfortable? This was a palace. She'd be just fine in the comforts of the guest room. What more could she possibly want?

Feya turned to face him as he started to close the door. His eyes landed on hers, and he stopped, leaving a one foot crack between the edge and the frame. She held his gaze, and something akin to fire filled his stomach. He felt her fear, and he couldn't stop the sympathy that swelled in his chest.

Strauth slammed the door. It seemed the only way to break the contact. He needn't feel for this woman. She and her family didn't deserve sympathy.

He inserted the key, and a soft click followed. Tracing his path back to the Great Hall, Strauth tried to erase the woman's terrified blue eyes from his mind, but they already haunted him. He and Ivrin would go with Aldeth in search of Morzaun. The distance was sure to free his conscious of them.

Strauth entered the hall and stood before Delran, who was firing a series of instructions to Aldeth and his family. "General Ivrin will accompany you, along with a dozen men of his choosing. He will share the details we have of Morzaun's last location, and he will also keep me informed of your every move. I want this handled as quickly as possible."

Delran turned his attention to Strauth. "Lieutenant, you will remain here to guard the girl."

His blood ran cold. "My King...you want me to stay here?"

"That is the assignment I desire for you."

"But—"

"General, please escort Aldeth and his family from the Great Hall so that I might have a private word with Lieutenant Strauth."

Ivrin passed Strauth a stern look and then did as the king asked. Once his brother and the magic wielders had all disappeared into the corridor, King Delran continued, "I know you aren't particularly fond of the assignment, Lieutenant, but allow me to explain my reasoning.

"I want no one else involved with these people. I don't trust them. For all I know, that girl could use her power to bewitch the servants—use them against their will. Such a thing would spell disaster. She will require tending to, and I'm asking you to take on the task and you alone. The fewer people she has contact with while she's here, the better. I trust you to see through any deceitful notions she might throw in your direction."

Strauth's forehead furrowed. Of course, the king's words were logical. He just wished he wasn't the one chosen for this assignment. He wanted to help track down Morzaun, not sit around the palace babysitting.

Delran placed his hand on Strauth's shoulder, startling him. "This doesn't come without opportunity. The moment they apprehend Morzaun, you will have access to this user of magic while her family is away. I'm quite confident you can find an opportunity to use this to your advantage. Also know that after this is over, you will have earned my highest respects."

His highest respect. To earn such sentiments from the king of Izarden and from his brother was the very thing Strauth had worked so hard to obtain these last few years. Gaining the position of lieutenant only months before had been the first step, but this would help him finally find his place.

And he needed a place. He needed to feel wanted...important. Essential.

He'd only felt that way once before—when his mother had taken ill. The sickness had rendered her completely helpless, and it had been Strauth who had taken care of her. The plague had lingered in her frail body for months before finally claiming the last of her energy. Though that time had been among the most difficult of his life, the experience of having someone rely upon him, need him, was one he couldn't forget.

His mother, though he knew she'd loved him, had been much like Ivrin in her reserved demeanor. She'd never hugged him—rarely touched him, for that matter—but he didn't need those things to have a fulfilling life. Strauth just needed to feel he had earned his place and had earned respect from those who mattered. Spending his nights alone in a cottage outside the palace walls spoke nothing to a fulfilling life.

Strauth nodded. "I understand, My King. I promise to perform my duties to the fullest."

"Very good, Lieutenant. We will talk more about this tomorrow. You are dismissed."

Strauth entered the corridor to find Ivrin waiting for him. "We're leaving right away," Ivrin said, keeping his voice low. "I know you wanted to come, but this may work to our advantage. I'll keep in touch with you. We'll figure out a way to continue with our plan."

Strauth gave him a firm nod. "Be careful in your travels, General."

His brother slipped closer to him, his eyes watching Aldeth and his family at the other end of the hall. "Be careful around the witch. She may try to sway you. Keep on your guard."

Ivrin pulled away and drew a deep breath. "Good evening, Lieutenant. Until we meet again."

CHAPTER SIX
First Impressions, Worst Impressions

The clear blue sky outside her window looked inviting, beckoning for her to come outside and explore the palace gardens. Feya closed her eyes and imagined the sun's gentle caress on her skin and the warmth of its rays flooding across it. On Verascene, she had spent most of her days basking in sunlight, picking flowers and lying on the soft green grass of the meadow. She'd never realized how much she would miss those carefree moments, and being trapped on an island suddenly held more appeal than it had before.

They'd come to Izarden, and somehow she'd still ended up trapped. Her tiny room in the palace was even more confining than Verascene. The door had been locked the moment that ruffian threw her inside, and she wondered if her entire visit to her family's old home would comprise locked doors. She hadn't slept all that well due to worrying over the situation, and any excitement she'd held for finally having the opportunity to travel had vanished.

Seeing the palace and walking its halls had been an interesting experience. Her emotions had become a tangled mess the moment they entered, and not just because of the meeting with King Delran. So much involving her family had happened between the white marble walls, and it was those events that had driven them to live on the island in the first place. Feya had been only a few months old when Delran's grandfather passed away and his son inherited the throne. Sytal had immediately asked her mother, father, and uncle to use their powers to assist him in his ploy for more power. Papa had always said Sytal was a greedy man, and his lust for control had thrown Izarden into conflict after conflict.

When her parents and uncle refused to be an instrument in the new king's plan of destruction, he'd exiled them from the kingdom. Magic was the only thing that had stood in the king's way, and to ensure those who used it did not thwart his designs of grandeur, he'd taken her uncle's wife as hostage. Aunt Senniva had been Sytal's sister, the princess of Izarden, but that hadn't stopped the man from threatening her. With her life in danger, her family agreed to leave, and Senniva remained behind under Sytal's watchful eye.

For eight years, Uncle Morzaun had lived on Verascene with them, away from his wife and son, who had been born after their departure. Her aunt and uncle corresponded through secret messages, and Senniva would often provide them with news on

Sytal's advances against neighboring kingdoms. Her father and uncle spent years spoiling the king's schemes, and those actions had likely saved many lives.

When Morzaun's son, Eramus, turned eight, he'd gained the ability to wield magic, just as she and her brothers could. Aunt Senniva managed to keep it a secret for several months, but after an incident involving a few guards, everything had crumbled.

Feya shook her head. She didn't want to think about the past. It only filled her with an overwhelming sadness. But with little else to do, keeping her thoughts in line was proving difficult.

Her stomach grumbled, and she rubbed it with furrowed brows. Did they intend to starve her? It wasn't as though she could leave and get her own food. Perhaps she should try the door again, not that she actually thought anyone would permit her to just wander the palace on her own.

She glided towards the door, but a few feet shy of it, the wood parted from its frame and slammed against the wall. Feya jumped backwards and squealed. She pressed her hand over her chest, where her heart threatened to break free.

Standing in the doorway, balancing a tray of food, was the man who'd brought her to the room yesterday. He wore the same black military uniform as he had the day before—one with gold cuffed sleeves and hints of purple on the seams—and the same scowl.

The only thing she knew about him was that he held the position of lieutenant and that he seemed to thoroughly despise her. Judging by the way he was glaring at her right now, that assumption still held merit.

But she refused to be intimidated by him.

Feya folded her arms and stuck out her chin. "Do you often barge into a lady's room without knocking? What if I had been sleeping, or perhaps changing?"

"Don't flatter yourself. Had I walked in on you changing, I simply would have retreated into the hall." His eyes fell over her, and her stomach lurched. "You offer little to entice my observation, so don't attempt to ensnare me with your conniving ways."

She gaped. Of all the impertinent things... She didn't have any desire to *ensnare* this man with anything, but still, his words hurt her pride. "Well, you don't exactly offer much of a view yourself." That wasn't true, of course. The man before her might be one of the most handsome she'd ever met. He needn't know that, though.

The lieutenant advanced and stopped just inches from her. Her pulse throbbed in her wrist. She met his eyes, and it took a great deal of self-control not to shrink under his scrutinizing gaze.

"Don't bother with whatever you're scheming, because it won't work on me," he said, before storming away from her and smacking the tray down on the desk near the window. The collision sent pieces of sausage to the floor and something splattering against the window. A thick gravy, she guessed, since its high viscosity kept it from running down to the window sill.

The man marched back to her, his cold voice piercing her like daggers. "Enjoy your breakfast, *witch*."

His words shouldn't have hurt. She shouldn't have cared. But she did. A witch defined her accurately, but it was his disdain that made her heart ache.

Feya turned away from him as her composure faltered. She fought the sting in her eyes and bit her lip to keep it from quivering. She hated that her magic poisoned people's impression of her before they could ever come to know who she really was. It came as no surprise, but that didn't mean his harsh words didn't deepen the already festering wound.

No, she wouldn't let him win. She wouldn't allow him under her skin.

Drawing on her inner strength, she returned her attention to the loathsome lieutenant, ready to fire an insult back at him, but she stopped herself. His expression had changed—softened. Regret lingered in his eyes only briefly, but she'd caught a glimpse before his brows tightened again.

"King Delran wishes to speak with you this afternoon," he said, in a dulcet tone she wouldn't have believed possible from him. "I'll return for you then."

He disappeared out the door and pulled it closed behind him. For several moments, she stared at the wooden entry, trying to sort out the perplexing interaction, and then her grumbling stomach reminded her of the reason the man had barged into her room in the first place. Feya sat down at the desk and began shoveling piles of eggs into her mouth, more famished than she'd realized.

She tried to push her encounter with the lieutenant from her mind, but too many questions pestered her to do so. Why in Virgamor was a lieutenant in Izarden's army bringing her breakfast? Surely he had more important things to do? She'd assumed the man would go with the general and her family in search of Morzaun.

Feya tapped the table with one finger, humming. The king must have ordered the man to play watch guard. He certainly hadn't seemed enthused about the assignment.

And neither was she.

She sighed and finished her breakfast. Hopefully, her family would find her uncle soon, and she wouldn't have to stay here long. Feya was certainly ready to go home. A few days in Izarden had shown her living on Verascene wasn't so bad after all. She couldn't stand the prejudice she had experienced. Living with it on a regular basis would be torturous.

Soft taps on her window garnered her attention. She withdrew from the desk and moved closer to the paned glass. A brown bird with auburn feathers tweeted noisily on the other side, dancing from side to side and pecking at the window every few seconds.

Feya smiled. Papa had a way with animals.

She pulled the knob and allowed the little creature to flutter inside. It landed on her desk, hopping with excitement. It held a small roll of parchment in its talons, which it dropped into Feya's hand when she held out her palm.

My dearest daughter,

I hope you will forgive me for abandoning you to stay at the palace. Had I thought there was any other way to forge peace between us and eliminate the hatred of Izarden's most noble in birth, I would not have done so. I reiterate my promise to find your uncle as quickly as we can. General Ivrin has a lead as to his whereabouts, and I hope it will provide us with success.

Your mother and I worry about how they will treat you. Though the king promised no harm would befall you, I admit my trust in him is only as deep as the shallows of Verascene. I'm certain they will not grant you parchment and quill, but if this letter finds you well, send it back with my friend so that I know you are all right.

Should I not receive it, I will come for you straight away. No pardon is worth the life of one of my most precious treasures.

With all my love,
Papa

Her entire body warmed. How she missed them already! What she wanted more than anything was to write the words her heart wished to say in response, but Papa was right. They had given her no parchment or quill. She could ask the lieutenant once he returned this afternoon, but that held more risk than she desired to take. Neither he nor the king would likely want her in correspondence with her family for fear they were conspiring against them. Their distrust ran too deep. If they found out Papa had contacted her, it could put their chance at a pardon in jeopardy.

Feya rolled the letter and handed it back to the bird, who had sung a cheery tune from the desk while she read. The little finch grasped it and hopped several times before taking flight out the window.

At least Papa would know she was all right, even if she couldn't write him a proper note. Thankfully, his powers gave him the ability to connect with animals; otherwise, she might have spent the entirety of her time in this palace prison wondering and worrying about her family.

She ran her fingers through her hair as she peered down into the courtyard below. The guest room overlooked the stone walkway from several stories above, much too high to jump.

Feya winced when her fingers snagged against a tangle. Her hair was a mess, and she had no way to remedy the issue. She and Zeeran had left everything in the barn, including the spare clothes they'd brought along for their journey. She had considered requesting the retrieval of their things, but she didn't want the king or anyone else to know where they'd been hiding. Papa's friend had been generous to allow them the use of his barn, and she feared what wrath he might incur if anyone found out.

She moseyed back to her bed and sat down. Why did Delran wish to speak with her, anyway? It didn't matter, she supposed. She wasn't much more than a prisoner at the moment. Worrying about it would do her little good, though she couldn't escape her thoughts with little else to do. She ought to think of a plan to escape, just in case the king decided to go back on his word, but right now, she felt too depleted to give the notion effort.

She lay down and wadded the soft blankets in her hands. At least her bed wasn't the hard ground she'd slept on the night before while they'd camped. Perhaps if she continued to look for the positives of being left behind, despite how scarce they were, she would manage the long days alone better.

Feya closed her eyes. Her mind drifted. A quick nap wouldn't be such a bad idea either.

CHAPTER SEVEN
Beautiful Distractions

Strauth marched to his window and spun on his heels. He headed back towards his door, and in seconds, he was at his window again. At this rate, his pacing might carve a trough in the floor. Mother had said he was like his father in that way. The moment Strauth grew anxious about something, he always defaulted into a steady parade back and forth across the room.

He ran his fingers through his hair as he made strides towards the door again. How in Virgamor was he going to do this? Why couldn't King Delran have just let him go with Ivrin? A low growl rumbled inside his throat. Perhaps if his new ward didn't possess a distracting beauty, he wouldn't have this problem. Why couldn't the witch look like an old hag?

No, instead she had long blonde hair that framed her face perfectly, even if it had been a bit of a mess. Somehow the woman pulled off the *just woke up* look in a way that made his heart skip a beat. He'd met his fair share of noble ladies over the past couple of years, many of which held a natural beauty, and yet somehow this woman had stolen his attention with one look.

One glaring look of disdain, as a matter of fact.

One thing was clear: they shared a dislike of one another. Of course, he hadn't exactly acted the gentleman. And he'd insulted her—twice.

That he felt guilty for it bothered him more than anything. The way her confidence had crumbled when he called her a *witch* still ate away at him, no matter how much his thoughts tried to justify that the word was accurate.

He wanted to eradicate magic, but causing pain to appear on her expression had cracked his resolve. After the fear she'd displayed the day before, he struggled to see her as the enemy, and right now, he couldn't afford to waver. Once Ivrin came up with a plan, he might expect Strauth to deal with her on his own.

Strauth stopped in the center of his room. The unfamiliar walls and furniture were doing nothing to ease his anxiety. His simple home outside the palace gate had always provided him comfort, even if he stayed there alone. Here, he only felt out of place.

He picked up his pacing again. What he needed was a solution. Perhaps if he just ignored Feya, he could manage until he heard from Ivrin. If he kept his mouth shut and refrained from insulting her, he wouldn't need to feel guilty, at least not until he—

Well, there was simply no need to think about that right now. When the time came to get his hands dirty, he would do his part and deal with the lady—witch. He would deal with the *witch*.

That was how he needed to think of her. He could manage that.

Something in the way his stomach twisted and his subconscious squirmed suggested he might be fooling himself. Despite his earlier confidence that this plan was both sound and warranted, doubt lingered, and he'd found no justification to completely extinguish it.

Strauth placed his hand on the metal knob and twisted. It was time to take the *witch* to see the king. What he desired to discuss with her, Strauth didn't know. He made his way down the corridor. His room was only a few doors down, which would prove convenient since Delran insisted Strauth be the only one to have contact with her. He'd be responsible for bringing her meals and escorting her should the king require, but Strauth figured his assignment wouldn't demand much more than delivering trays of food. The less he saw of the magic wielder, the better, especially if he planned to ignore her.

He paused at her door. She'd chided him for not knocking this morning, but one didn't knock on a prisoner's door. Even if they were a lady—witch. He growled at his uncooperative thoughts.

With a quick turn of the rounded brass, he threw open the entry, banging it against the interior wall, and stepped inside. She jumped, just as she had last time, and shot him a scowl.

"Must you slam the door? If you refuse to knock, you could at least try to not scare me."

Perhaps she was ri—no. Strauth strode forward, keeping a watchful eye on her. She might decide to use her magic on him, and he needed to be ready.

Not that he could do much about it if she did.

"It's time to meet with the king." She gave no response, and after some hesitation, he wrapped his hand around her arm.

Her muscles tensed beneath his fingers, but she didn't refuse his guidance to the door. Strauth kept his gaze focused on the path ahead. He could handle this. He would take her to see Delran and bring her straight back. No conversation necessary.

"What does the king want?" she asked in a whisper.

"You'll find out soon enough," he answered, his words clipped. Strauth swallowed and stole a quick side glance. She displayed that terrified look again. Why did someone capable of using magic possess so much fear? And why did *he* feel compelled to reassure her she needn't be afraid?

Ridiculous notion.

It wasn't as though he knew what Delran wanted, anyway. The king had given him an order. Questions weren't necessary to obey them.

"Will you be going with me to see him?" Her voice quivered, and he drew her to a stop just outside the stone archway into the Great Hall. The two guards eyed them, hands tight on the hilts of their sheathed swords.

Strauth glanced down at the witch. It was only now that he realized she trembled in his grasp. Perhaps Aldeth had put on the act of a gentleman, but this—this terror was genuine.

"Of course I'll go with you. You don't think we'd actually allow a witch to see the king alone?"

She winced, and his stomach knotted. He hadn't meant for his tone to sound as harsh as it did, but the way she befuddled his emotions had him frustrated.

"I suppose from your perspective that wouldn't be logical," she said. "Magic can be dangerous."

He shifted. Her agreeing with him only confused him further...and made him more uncomfortable.

Strauth led her into the Great Hall, passing the four guards posted just inside the door and giving them a quick nod. Delran sat on his golden throne, slouched sideways with his head propped up on his fist. He straightened when he noticed their approach. Strauth brought Feya to stand before the king and released her arm to dip into a low bow. She followed his example with a wobbly curtsy.

"Feya, isn't it?" asked Delran, looking her over as he had Strauth the day before.

"Yes, Your Highness."

"Have you found your sleeping quarters comfortable, Feya?"

She clasped her hands in front of her and rested her gaze on the floor. "Of course, Your Highness. You are most generous for granting me a place in your guest wing."

"Very good. Well, I've called you here to establish some rules for your stay at the palace. As you can imagine, the presence of a magic wielder produces a bit of restlessness among my people and, more specifically, my staff. To keep the situation as pleasant as possible,

I've asked my lieutenant to...see to your needs. You are to have contact with no one but him."

"No one?" she squeaked, jerking her head up to look at him. Delran lifted a brow, and Feya quickly continued. "Forgive me, Your Highness. It's just that...well, if there is *anyone* else who might—"

"I've appointed someone I trust and whom I believe will keep you safe should the need arise. Are you not satisfied with my choice?"

She lifted her chin, just as she had when Strauth entered her room this morning. His lips twitched. Her haughty facade amused him, and he gave her credit for at least trying to put on a brave face.

"No. I'm not satisfied, My King. Safe is certainly not how I feel with this"—she paused and stole a glance at Strauth—"*lieutenant.*"

His title hadn't been what she'd wanted to say—that was clear—but what had she planned to call him instead? This morning, she'd wanted to repay his insult. He'd seen it in her pinched expression. But she had refrained, and it seemed she'd done so again. His curiosity burned annoyingly bright.

Delran growled and tapped his fingers against his throne. "You don't feel safe with a man of such high rank? Do you not believe he possesses the skill to protect you? Or perhaps you think yourself above the need with your powers?"

"I do not think myself above it." She turned to Strauth. He'd expected to see anger in her eyes, but they only contained a treacherous sadness that stabbed at his heart. "I'm sure the lieutenant is perfectly adept, but capability and willingness are not the same things."

She didn't think him willing to defend her? She was right to assume such a thing, of course, seeing as how he intended to take out her and her family. Still, her words pierced him. The idea of anyone having such little faith in him only reaffirmed how useless he often felt. Ivrin didn't need him. The king could replace him in a heartbeat. Strauth was not indispensable.

"I'm afraid your opinion is of little consequence to me, Miss Feya. And since you will spend most of your time in your room, it makes little difference, regardless. You are not permitted to wander the corridors or to leave the palace. You may only leave your quarters under escort, and by my permission. This is to protect both you and my people, you understand. We wouldn't want any harm to befall you, nor for your *powers* to inflict damage on anyone or anything else. I hope I have made myself clear on the matter?"

Her expression fell, and an irrational disappointment filled Strauth at her loss of spirit. "Yes, Your Highness."

"Very well. You may return her to her chamber, Lieutenant."

Strauth bowed and took Feya by the arm again. As they passed through the stone arch, his mind raced. He was growing tired of the guilt this witch planted in his chest. He hated magic, and therefore, he had to hate those who wielded it. His father had died because of them, and no matter how innocent Feya seemed, she was a threat to all of Virgamor.

Wasn't she?

They turned the corner, and for the first time Feya countered his pull. He turned to face her.

"Let me go. I can walk on my own!" She jerked, and Strauth had to tighten his hold to not lose her. She pried at his fingers.

"The king ordered you to your room. Stop resisting!"

"Let go!" Her fingers dug between his, and she used all her body weight to pull against him as he attempted to move forward. Strauth was half tempted to throw her over his shoulder and carry her back. But he just needed to round one more corner...

"Lieutenant!" His feet came to a halt, and he met her fierce gaze—one he somehow felt both intimidated by and admired. How did someone so tiny manage such a thing? "You're hurting my arm," she said, her tone calm but stern. "Let. Me. Go."

Hurting her? He hadn't meant to, but her struggle had tightened his grip more than he'd realized. Strauth released his hold, and her hand immediately moved to cover the offended area.

"I didn't mean to—"

"I know you despise me, but if you could find it in yourself to allow me the smallest respite from your hatred, I promise to remain compliant."

Strauth's brows furrowed. Why her statement of the obvious bothered him, he couldn't say. She believed he despised her. Hated her.

And he did.

Or at least he was trying very hard to. Why the devil did that look in her eyes twist his insides like vines covering a lattice?

He heaved a sigh and reached toward her. "Come."

She flinched away from his touch, and the reaction made his stomach roll. He eased his hand closer, meeting the sleeve of her purple dress. Instead of wrapping his fingers around her arm, he merely applied a gentle pressure to the fabric. "Please, come."

Surprise stole over her expression, which bothered him more than he cared to admit. He hadn't acted the gentleman with her, but the desire to show he could be one overwhelmed him. Strauth needn't prove himself to the girl, but good Virgamor he desperately wanted to.

She allowed him to guide her back to her room, and when they reached the door, he opened it for her like any honorable man would.

Feya entered and then spun around to look at him. "Thank you."

The words made him squirm. Thank you? Why did she feel compelled to thank him? Whatever the reason, he was in serious jeopardy of losing his breakfast from the way his stomach felt. Perhaps he was taking ill.

Strauth tapped his fingers against his leg. She no longer held her arm, but...

"I apologize for causing you pain. Does it still hurt?"

She shook her head. "I'll survive."

Of course she would. She was much stronger than her petite frame would lead anyone to believe. "I'll try to be less—"

"Barbaric?"

"That wasn't the word I was going to use, but I suppose it could be applied."

"Perhaps reprehensible is better?"

Strauth cocked his brow. She certainly wasn't holding back her insults now. He may as well let her finish. "Anything else?"

"I could name a few, but I don't think my father would approve of them coming from his daughter."

Strauth pursed his lips to suppress a smile. "I've enough imagination to figure them out."

She folded her arms, displaying a look of satisfaction that nearly made him laugh. "Good."

"Good," he agreed. "I will see you at dinner, then."

"If you insist."

"Of course I do."

Her stern expression faltered just long enough for him to catch a glimpse of a grin. Strauth gave his hand a dramatic flourish and bowed before pulling the door closed.

What in Virgamor was he doing? He wasn't supposed to be talking to Feya, let alone flirting with her.

Strauth inserted the key, and made his escape to his own quarters. He needed a distraction, and one that wasn't so perplexing, witty, and attractive. Perhaps he should lie down before this sickness became any worse.

CHAPTER EIGHT

An Almost Escape

Feya smoothed out the folds in the blanket on her bed and sat down. Part of her wanted to lie down and slip into a deep sleep, but her troubled heart wouldn't allow it. The king's words floated repeatedly across her mind, breaking her spirit more with each pass. So long as she remained at the palace, her world would mostly comprise the four walls surrounding her. King Delran had attempted to convince her it was, in part, for her own safety, but she wasn't naïve. He only cared about keeping her magic under his thumb.

She had known prior to their journey that the people of Izarden despised magic, but their animosity had far exceeded her expectations. To be the subject of such disdain ripped her soul. She couldn't blame the people for their fear, and their hatred wasn't necessarily misplaced. Her uncle had destroyed so many lives, and Feya wanted to be nothing like him.

But her uncle hadn't always been that way. He'd once believed in using his power to help the people. One moment of emotional chaos had pushed him down a dark path. He'd lost control of his magic, and it was that very thing that Feya feared most. She refused for that to happen to her, which meant she needed to keep her power in line, and the easiest way to do so was to not use magic at all.

She exhaled on a shaky breath. Days on end inside this room with no one to talk to might unravel her completely. She'd never felt so alone. As far back as her memories would take her, Feya had always had her family. Her brothers, though often the bane of her existence, had been her constant companions. Her mother and father had been her comfort and guidance throughout her youth. Without them, her mind panicked in a labyrinth of hopeless thoughts. How would she manage this trial without them?

Feya rose from the bed and sauntered closer to the window. Perhaps Papa would continue to send her letters. Even if she couldn't respond, hearing from him would help her weather this internal storm. He'd stated that General Ivrin had a lead on her uncle's whereabouts. If it proved fruitful, her family might not be gone long at all. Then they could return home.

But what if the general's tip didn't pay off? What if it took weeks to track down Morzaun? Months, even? Her heart rate quickened.

She wasn't sure she could handle that. Feya needed her family. She needed to consider an alternative to waiting around for them to return.

She peered out the window at the ground below. The first thing she'd considered after being tossed into the room was whether a window escape was possible. At this height, jumping proved out of the question, but maybe if she could climb down...

Bunching the velvet blankets in her hands did nothing to ease her constricted lungs. She felt like she might suffocate. If she left, any chance of a pardon would go with her, but Feya wasn't sure she could stay. Delran hadn't directly threatened her, but she could sense his disdain, and she certainly didn't trust the man.

Papa would understand. He'd told her in the quietest whisper before the lieutenant had hauled her from the Great Hall that she was to go back to the barn should she feel threatened. Feya had thought she could ignore the hatred directed at her, but the weight of it suffocated her. What good would a pardon do if the people of Izarden looked at them with such disgust?

Feya spun around, her eyes scanning the room for a solution. Her tiny prison held little promise. She had a bed, a table with two chairs, and a wardrobe with nothing inside. She tapped her finger to her chin as she made a lap around the room, and she slid her hand across the soft blanket of her bed when she passed.

The blankets!

In a rush of waving limbs, she ripped the sheets from the four-poster bed and tossed them in a pile on the floor. If she knotted them together, she could use them to climb down. But would they hold her?

She shook her head and got to work. This was a room in the palace. If any sheets stood a chance, it was these—the most finely crafted bedding in the kingdom. Besides, they were her only option. If she had any hope of escape, they would have to do.

Her fingers worked quickly, placing the ends together and twisting them into a knot. The sun already hung low on the horizon, and in order to pull this off successfully, she needed to finish before the loathsome lieutenant returned with her dinner tray. Feya would have no quarrel with never seeing *that* man again.

She bit her lip, her brows furrowing. He hadn't been kind to her at first, but their last interaction had been different. The brief guilt she'd seen on his face this morning had flooded his expression once again when she'd made him aware that his stubborn hold on her arm while escorting her from the Great Hall had brought her pain. His tone had changed. He'd asked her to follow with a please and a soft hand after that, both of which had taken her by complete surprise. He'd even seemed amused by their banter at her door. Though he tried desperately to hide it, she suspected a good man existed below that rough, sour surface. Shame he didn't offer that version of himself to her.

Feya pulled the last knot into place and headed for the window. With the lift of the handle, the warm subtropical air greeted her, sweeping across her skin. She closed her eyes. Freedom lay just beyond those marble walls, and she would take it. She'd hide in the barn until Papa and her family returned. Surely he would look for her there the moment he received word that she'd escaped?

She slipped back to the bed and tied one end of her salvation around the nearest post. She gave it a heavy pull. The furniture squeaked against the floor, and she stopped. If someone heard, the sound would draw the attention of the palace guards to investigate. Feya slowly worked the bed towards the wall, moving each post in turn and keeping her constant pad around the bed as quiet as possible.

Once the furniture rested by the window, she gave a peek into the courtyard below. A guard ambled across the stone pavers, whistling a cheery tune. He disappeared from her view around the corner of the palace and she wadded her makeshift rope in her lap, waiting. Every few minutes, the guard would reappear, walking in the opposite direction. After a few rounds, she had his timing down to a few seconds. She was ready.

The second the guard vanished behind the white wall, Feya thrust the sheets over the edge. The knotted strand of fabric hung nearly to the ground. She smiled and slid onto the windowsill. The height made her stomach lurch into her throat, but she didn't have time to be afraid. She gripped the sheet and began her descent.

She'd made it halfway down the wall when a ripping sound echoed from the window ledge, followed by a vibration through the sheet. Feya froze. Perhaps she *had* overestimated the strength of the fine palace linens. What should she do? She was still high enough that a fall might cause her serious harm, but she didn't relish the idea of climbing back up and falling from an even greater height should the sheets not hold.

Whistling caught her ears. Her stomach twisted. This situation was nothing but bad news. What had she been thinking?

She held her breath as the guard approached, walking several yards in front of the wall she was nestled against. He kept his focus on his path forward, occasionally ceasing his high-pitched blowing to add words in a baritone hum.

Once he passed around the corner, she inhaled. She'd gotten lucky, but Feya wouldn't wager on another round of fortune. She lowered herself slowly, but another rip left her frozen again.

A loud smack reverberated from inside her room, and she glanced up. Her heart pounded. She had company, and one that wouldn't be happy with her whereabouts. The loathsome lieutenant appeared in her view seconds later, peering over the edge of the windowsill, and a deep scowl filled his expression when his eyes met hers.

"What do you think you're doing!"

Indeed, that was a good question.

She'd been so desperate to escape that she had exaggerated her chances of success. The notion had seemed easy from the safety of her chamber. What a horrible plan she'd contrived.

"Climb back up here immediately!" shouted the lieutenant, his tone a mixture of irritation and concern.

"I can't!"

Her reply only deepened his scowl. His hands moved to the sheet, and he pulled.

"No! Don—"

The word became lost to her as the sheet ripped completely and sent her barreling towards the ground along with her screams. Feya crashed against the pavers, landing on her foot. Her knees buckled at the collision and her hands, attempting to catch her fall, scratched against the rough stone. Specs of crimson spread across the white marble and her foot throbbed. She curled into a ball against the cold ground, clutching her ankle and gritting her teeth.

Fast approaching boots clicked against the stone path. A shadow fell over her. "What is this? Aren't you that witch who's supposed to be locked up in the palace?"

She recognized the deep voice of the man who'd been whistling and singing only minutes before. "Maybe you ought to be thrown in the dungeon if you don't appreciate our hospitality." The words, laced with venom, only added to the physical pain she already felt. Fingers brushed over her arm, and the man lifted her. The movement fired pain up her leg, making her scream.

"Please let go!"

The man sneered and dragged her a few yards before she crumbled back to the ground. He reached down to pull her up again.

"Hands off her!"

She recognized that voice, too. The lieutenant marched towards them, his breathing heavy from what Feya guessed had been a mad dash from her chamber. "I was just going to take her to the dungeons," said the guard. "She clearly needs a set of bars instead of a comfortable room."

"That isn't for you to decide."

The guard, who appeared much older than the lieutenant, puffed up his chest. "Well, maybe I ought to speak to someone a little more sensible? Keeping this witch around is a danger for us all. Why not just eliminate her while she has no one around for protection?"

He pulled on her arm again, and she groaned as more pain burned through her foot. The lieutenant grabbed the guard by his collar. "I said let her go. That's an *order.*"

The guard glared, but loosened his grip until she slipped from his grasp.

"You would do well to remember who your superiors are," said the lieutenant, thrusting a finger into the man's inflated chest. "Or perhaps it will be you who is thrown into the dungeon. No one is to deal with her but me, and I expect your silence about this incident. Is that clear?"

"Yes, sir."

"Good. Now resume your post."

The guard bowed and disappeared from her view. Not that she could see much the way her eyes pinched at the pain exploding from her ankle. Fingers wrapped around her upper arm, and brought her to her feet—briefly. Her legs refused to hold her with the sharp pain, and she crumpled against the lieutenant with another groan. He let her fall to his feet.

Feya gripped her injured foot and winced just as his bearded face appeared beside her. His eyes darted from hers to where she held her ankle. "I know you're capable of healing yourself, so take care of your injury."

Her heart skipped a beat. "I—"

"That isn't a request."

She swallowed and waved her hands over her foot. The words to the *sanarus* flowed from her lips. Sparks of purple light flickered between her palms, but that's where the magic ended. Desperation filled her. She whirled her hands frantically, reciting the incantation several times, to no avail.

"What's taking so long?"

His clipped words did nothing to help. Feya gave the attempt one last try without success. Tears streamed from her eyes, and she left her hands hovering over her ankle. "I can't...I can't use my magic."

She had expected to hear his frustrated voice descend upon her again, but instead silence filled the small gap between them. With a shaky breath, she dared to glance at him. His brows had furrowed, but with confusion rather than anger.

"I can't use magic," she repeated, choking out the statement. Perhaps he hadn't heard her properly. Not being able to heal her own injuries was sure to, at minimum, annoy the man.

He studied her for several moments, as if trying to work out the truth of her words. Without warning, one strong arm wrapped around her waist and the other swooped under her legs, scooping her against his chest. The maneuver made her gasp, bringing with it a deep inhale filled with his woody scent.

The hand not tucked against him gripped his uniform. She didn't dare look at him. Her entire body trembled, but Feya had no fear of being dropped. Whether she liked the lieutenant or not, she couldn't deny his sculpted form left her undoubting of his capability for the task.

What worried her was the questions the man would ask. She didn't enjoy discussing her lack of current ability with her family, let alone a stranger. Not only that, but divulging her paucity of power would pin a target on her back. If the people of Izarden learned just how vulnerable she was, they might make an attempt on her life, and something told her there would be no one to protect her from such a threat.

Then again, someone *had* just protected her from the guard, but whether it was out of duty to his assignment or genuine concern, she didn't know.

Regardless, Feya had spilled her secret, all because she had thought herself capable of self rescue. What a joke that had turned out to be. She was completely helpless, even more so now with her injuries. One thing was certain—she wouldn't be attempting another escape, especially when it put her in the arms of a man who hated her.

CHAPTER NINE
Negotiating with the Enemy

Strauth's heart raced, and he wondered if the hand that gripped his coat could feel just how hard it pounded. An attempted escape was the last thing he would have expected from the petite body in his arms. A fall from such a height could have been much worse, and the witch was lucky her injuries weren't more severe.

The *witch*.

Perhaps that word wasn't as accurate as he had once thought. Yes, purple sparks had emanated from her palms when she had tried to heal herself, and she had spoken in a language that sounded foreign to his ears, but nothing had come from the effort. She'd said she couldn't use magic, and from what he could tell, she hadn't lied.

The expression of pain that graced her face each time she moved confirmed as much. No one would sit in that kind of torment if they had the means to fix it.

That she'd shared such a sensitive truth only confused him. The information brought with it too many questions, ones he would need to know the answers to. Such details would be important in his mission to eradicate magic.

Strauth rounded the corner to the guest wing. Feya's breaths came in shaky gasps, and her body trembled against his. The urge to hold her tighter nearly overwhelmed him, but he stopped his muscles before they could do so. Why in Virgamor did she evoke such feelings in him?

He entered her room and closed the door with his foot. The last thing he needed was the servants catching wind of what had happened. Should Delran find out he had almost failed in his assignment, it wouldn't bode well for Strauth. He set Feya down on her bed, and she released her grip on his coat. A quick glance over her reminded him that she had scraped her hand after her fall. The scratches weren't bad but would still need to be cleaned.

"Wait right here," he said, putting more warning in his tone than was probably necessary. She likely wouldn't attempt to escape again right now, and even if she did, the woman wouldn't get far, judging by the ways she still grimaced in pain. "I'll be back in a moment."

She never looked at him, never said a word. Strauth marched from the room and pulled the door closed behind him.

He returned just a few minutes later with a bowl of water, a rag, and some linen for bandaging. Her wounds required tending, and since Strauth was the only one permitted to have contact with her, that left the job to him. He groaned inwardly. His title should mean this type of assignment fell beneath him, but apparently that wasn't the case.

Something squashed beneath his boot, and he grimaced. In his rush to stop her escape, he'd dropped Feya's dinner tray, spilling the contents all over the floor. He'd have to clean that up too.

Strauth set the water and linens on the small table—which was now right next to the bed since she had pushed the furniture towards the window—and crouched in front of her. Feya finally lifted her gaze, revealing her tear-studded face. His frustration melted. Could he really blame her for trying to run away? He hadn't exactly treated her with kindness, and the whole situation obviously terrified her.

"Which foot hurts?"

She blinked at him for a moment and then pointed to her right. Strauth lifted the hem of her dress just enough to reveal a pair of brown leather boots. She certainly had small feet. They matched the rest of her, he supposed.

He slipped the boot from her foot. Why the action made his pulse erratic, he didn't know. Taking her ankle with both hands, he pressed his fingers along the bones. She winced and wadded a handful of her dress in her palm, smearing blood over the purple fabric. When he dug deeper, her hand shot to his arm, accompanying a gasp.

Strauth glanced at where her hand met his sleeve—where his skin prickled beneath the fabric and her fingertips. "Forgive me. I'm only checking to see if it's broken."

Forgive him? Confound his befuddled emotions. He needn't apologize to her. He shouldn't even need to deal with this in the first place. She placed her hand back into her lap. Strauth cleared his throat and rose. "It isn't broken, but you'll need to stay off of it for a few days. At least until the swelling has gone down."

Strauth dipped the rag into the bowl of water. The chair squeaked against the floor when he moved it closer to her and sat down. She watched him intently but still didn't say a word. He couldn't help but wonder what she was thinking. He should probably scold her for what had happened, but he couldn't bring himself to do it.

He reached for her wrist—the one streaked with blood—and his touch made her flinch. Feya tucked her hand against her stomach.

Her distrust of him made his insides squirm.

"I just want to clean your wounds," he said, keeping his tone soft. "That's all."

Her brows furrowed, and she dropped her gaze to where her hands rested. "You're not...you're not angry with me?"

Was he angry with her? He searched himself for the emotion that should have been there but found no contempt. Her actions frustrated him, sure. Strauth didn't particularly enjoy playing doctor any more than he enjoyed babysitting, but he couldn't say he felt angry. At least not about this.

"No, I'm not angry with you."

Her shoulders slumped a little. Perhaps if he kept her talking, she would let him finish. Then he could leave, because that's what he wanted—peace and quiet, so he could sort out his thoughts. Strauth held out his hand, palm up. Maybe if he let her come to him, she wouldn't be so afraid.

Feya stared at his outstretched hand for several seconds before lifting her own. She hesitantly placed it into his, and a wave of chills surged through his body, making him tense. He used his thumb to hold back her fingers, exposing the scrapes on her palm, and gently dabbed the wet rag over the area. She flinched when he reached the worst of her wounds, subconsciously jerking her hand, but Strauth tightened his fingers around hers, keeping her from slipping away.

"I don't blame you for trying to escape," he said, hoping the conversation would distract her until he finished. "If I were in your place, I imagine I would have done the same thing."

She scowled and shook her head. "If you were in my place, you would have succeeded in escaping, not failed miserably like me."

Strauth suppressed a smile. "I don't believe those sheets capable of bearing my weight any better than they did yours."

"I suppose that's true. Using them for my prison break wasn't the wisest of decisions. Do you have any better suggestions for my next attempt?"

Next attempt? He stopped cleaning the blood from her hand and met her gaze with a frown. She giggled and turned away.

Ah. She was teasing him.

When she faced him again, he gave her a pointed look and began wrapping the linen around her hand. "Your cuts aren't deep. They should heal just fine."

"How is it that a lieutenant has so much experience tending to injuries?"

He shrugged. "I've been in Izarden's army for seven years. Seen my fair share of accidents. I suppose I picked up a thing or two. And I've only been a lieutenant for a few months."

Strauth tied off her bandage and swooped forward to pick her up, not giving her a chance to protest. She gasped, gripping his coat once again. He didn't move her far, just to the other chair next to the table, and she looked at him with wide eyes when he sat her down.

"What are you doing?" she asked, a deep line appearing across her forehead. "Why did you pick me up again?"

"Perhaps I just enjoy carrying helpless damsels such as yourself about the palace."

She gaped, and he spun around before she could catch sight of his grin. Strauth slipped to the window and pulled what remained of the sheets back inside. He untied them from the bedpost and gave the furniture several shoves to position it back where it was supposed to be.

Strauth folded his arms and lifted his brows. "I'll go find you some new bedding, but only if you promise not to ruin them."

Her expression fell, and she rubbed her thumb across the cloth on her injured hand. "Do you intend to tell King Delran about this?"

Fear had found its way into her voice again. Strauth sighed and approached her. His hand met her waist, and the other slid under her knees. The maneuver didn't surprise her as much this time, but she still kept a firm grip on his coat as he moved her back to the bed. Why *was* he picking her up again, anyway? She could have limped the short distance. It must have been his ingrained expectation to act like a gentleman. That, and the way it startled her amused him.

"I'll make you deal," he said, slipping his arms out from under her. "If you agree not to attempt escaping again, then I'll agree not to tell the king." Not that he intended to anyway. Delran didn't need to know he'd almost failed at his duty.

"I accept," she said so hastily it almost brought out a chuckle from him.

Strauth shook his head. "Oh, no. This is far too serious for just words. If we are to make a deal, it must be done properly."

She narrowed her eyes when he stepped closer. "And how do we do so *properly*?"

"First you must square your shoulders, sit up straight, and look me right in the eyes." He scooted the chair over to the bed, and taking a seat, waited for her to follow his instructions. She executed them to perfection and added her haughty chin lift to finish.

Strauth was at risk of losing his composure. He'd never worked so hard to hold back a laugh. "Good. Now, you must state the terms of our agreement, and then, we will shake on it."

Feya dropped her gaze to what he guessed were the buttons on his coat. "I, Feya, agree—"

"Ah! Eyes." Strauth used two fingers to point to his own. "That part is important. My father always said you can tell if a man is true to his word by his eyes."

Her nose wrinkled with her smile. "I should like to think myself a man true to my word, but I may be failing terribly at half of that statement."

Strauth covered the burst of laughter with a cough. "Then we'd best make sure you don't fail at the other half."

She began again, her gaze firmly connected with his own. "I, Feya, agree to put my unsatisfactory attempts at escaping behind me."

"And I agree to keep the details of said unsatisfactory attempts to myself."

Strauth held out his hand, but Feya hesitated to take it. "I have one more stipulation," she whispered, her expression sheepish. "I'd like to know your name."

His name? All this time she hadn't even known his name? Of course she didn't. He hadn't taken the time to exchange pleasantries with her. Guilt shouldn't have nagged at him, but it did. "Strauth," he answered.

She took his hand, giving it a firm shake, and something danced inside his stomach. "I accept your terms, Lieutenant Strauth."

"And I yours, Miss Feya."

The agreement was made. He could have released her hand. She could have pulled away. But neither of them moved. He'd never felt so trapped in someone's gaze. Part of him felt the need to fight it, for fear he might drown, and the other part wanted to stay there, content to remain lost in the sea of blue before him.

He dropped her hand when she looked away. What in Virgamor was the matter with him? Just this morning, he had insulted her and decided to completely ignore the witch—Feya. Her name was Feya. He couldn't think of her as the former anymore, not now that he knew her secret. The thought only reminded him of all the questions swirling around in the back of his mind. He wanted to ask them, but he also felt an urgency to get out of that room.

"I'll bring you a new set of sheets and some clean rags to wash up," he said, standing. His questions would have to wait until he sorted himself out. "Then you should rest."

Strauth turned to leave, but his name melodically riding her voice pulled him to a stop. "Strauth?" He turned to look at her over his shoulder, and she offered him a small smile, one that sent feathers floating about inside his stomach. "Thank you."

His lips lifted before he could stop them. "You're welcome."

Confound it; he needed to get out of there.

Strauth exited her room and locked the door. He had to put an end to this. From now on, he needed to ignore her. The idea was simple enough, but his gut told him the endeavor would prove far more difficult than he planned. His walls were crumbling, and he hadn't the slightest idea how to keep them standing.

CHAPTER TEN
Twisted Truths

The courtyard below her window was devoid of any movement. Feya hadn't seen a guard pass by since the storm had begun. Dark clouds filled the sky, and the smell of rain permeated through the small crack of the open window, a space just big enough to allow her to catch a waft of the fresh earthy scent without getting wet. The soft patters of the storm lulled her into closing her eyes.

Verascene often saw many storms, and this one only made her miss home even more. With nothing else to focus on, her thoughts wandered through her memories, making her heart ache. The last three days had been miserable.

Feya turned to take in her empty room. Loneliness pricked at her soul. She hadn't heard from Papa again and wondered if they were close to locating her uncle. She missed her family desperately, and despite knowing they had magic to protect them, worried over their well-being. Their powers didn't make them invincible, and Feya didn't trust the general or his men to value her family's life.

Her eyes fell on the long mirror leaning against the wall on the opposite side of the room. Her hair was a mess again, strands sticking out every which way. She had spent time the last few days weaving her fingers through them, but the desire had deserted her. What was the point? There was only one person who ever saw her, and it wasn't as though he cared. In fact, he'd made sure she understood he saw nothing attractive in her appearance.

Her hair wasn't the only thing in a complete disaster. A small streak of red coated her purple dress, a bloodstain from her failed attempt at escaping. With nothing to change into, she supposed she'd just have to deal with wearing the constant reminder. Her hand had mostly healed, with only a few rough scabs remaining, and she no longer wore the linen bandage, but her foot still ached, leaving her with a bit of a limp. Still, she was lucky her injuries hadn't been worse, and she was fortunate that the lieutenant had been willing to tend to the ones she'd sustained.

Those few minutes with him had given her hope. He'd been cordial with her, at least more so than before. They'd even teased one another. For a moment, she'd thought she wouldn't have to spend her entire time in the palace alone with no one to talk to, but she'd been wrong. Three days had come and gone since then, and

Lieutenant Strauth hadn't spoken one word to her. He entered four times each day to deliver her meals and later retrieve her tray—and take care of other unpleasantries that would normally fall to a maid—and each time she'd offered him a polite smile. He'd only returned his typical sour expression and quickly marched from her room.

She wasn't naïve. She knew he still despised her, but she had allowed herself a false hope, and now it tore her apart.

Feya closed the window and flipped the latch into place. She rested her head against the cold glass, feeling as dreary on the inside as the storm made Izarden appear.

The door flung open and smacked against the wall. Having grown used to the lieutenant's grandiose arrivals, Feya kept her gaze on the courtyard. She didn't budge when he set a new tray of food down on the little wooden table next to her. In seconds, the door would close again, and that would be that.

But the sound never came. From the corner of her eye, she could see Strauth's tall form facing her. Why hadn't he left? She reined in her desire to look at him.

"Are you all right?" His soft voice broke both the silence and her resolve. She turned to look at him and found concern spread over his face. She lifted her brows in question, and he shifted. "You didn't smile at me."

Feya folded her arms. "I wasn't aware smiling every time you walked into the room was a requirement. You certainly never seemed to appreciate it before now."

"I don't," he said, but something in the way his brows pinched made her wonder if that were true. "I just thought something might be wrong since you didn't."

"I'm a prisoner in this room with absolutely no one to talk to. What could possibly be wrong?" She turned back to the window. She wouldn't waste a smile on someone like him. Not anymore.

His boots tapped against the floor as he made his way to the door, and she breathed a sigh of relief when it closed with a thud. It was short-lived, however. Not a minute later, the door bounced off the wall again, and Lieutenant Strauth paraded inside. He placed a second tray on her table and plopped down on the chair.

"What are you doing?" she asked.

"Eating breakfast, which is what you should be doing."

She scoffed. "And *why* are you eating breakfast in here? You've never done so before."

He swallowed his food and met her gaze. "If I eat here, I don't have to come back for your tray. Saves me a trip."

Feya slid off the bench that rested beneath her window, knocking one of the round cushions to the floor, and glared at him. "And what if I'm not ready to eat right this second? Or perhaps don't want to take my meal with *you*?"

He leaned forward on his elbows and lifted one brow. Feya's heart stuttered. Why did her guard have to be so devilishly handsome?

"Then I will return your tray full of food to the kitchen, and I imagine you'll be far more inclined to eat your dinner later this evening."

Were it not for the smell of warm baked biscuits, perhaps she would have let him do just that, but her grumbling stomach argued too thoroughly for her to refuse. Feya hobbled to the table, keeping weight off her injured ankle. It still hurt anytime she applied pressure to it. She sank into her chair and heaved a dramatic sigh. Strauth's lips lifted with a quick twitch.

For several minutes, they ate in silence.

"How's your foot?" he asked, without lifting his gaze from his tray.

She dropped her spoon, still full of eggs, and stared at him. "There's no need for the façade, Lieutenant."

"And what façade might that be?"

"That you care."

Deep lines embedded in his forehead. "Would I have tended to your injuries if I didn't?" The question came laced with more than just sarcasm. Something in the way he said it made her wonder if he were actually asking himself rather than her.

"I don't know," she answered. "The king assigned you as my guard. What responsibilities that entails is open for interpretation, and I suspect you wouldn't have helped me if not for your duty."

"That's not—" he began, but stopped himself and rubbed a hand over his beard. Strauth jumped up from his chair so suddenly she started. The man paced from one side of her room to the other, running a hand through his dirty blond locks and leaving them less orderly than she'd ever seen them.

Did her words bother him *that* much? He stopped in the center of the room and turned to face her as she stood. "Why can't you use your magic?"

The question sent her heart into her throat. She'd suspected he would ask, but had thought after having avoided it the last few days that she'd escaped the conversation. Feya bit her lip. He already knew about her lack of ability; explaining the cause wouldn't do any more harm.

"Because I'm afraid of it," she answered, just above a whisper.

His face contorted. "You're afraid of your own power? Why?"

She drew a deep breath. She didn't owe him an explanation, but things would be easier if they just got it out of the way. Besides, the reprieve from her constant loneliness was nice, even if it came from someone she knew hated her.

"I don't want to be like my uncle. He used his power to hurt so many people. At one time, he was a good man—a man who wanted to help the people of Izarden. But now—"

"He's a murderer."

She nodded. "I'm afraid of my power, of losing control of it."

"And you think by not using it you're different?" Strauth's eyes, so like the gray clouds outside Feya's window, held a storm of their own. "Magic corrupts the soul. It leads to nothing but chaos and destruction. Morzaun is a murderer and so is your father. Anyone who possesses such darkness could be little else."

"My father is not a murderer!" She stood, clenching her fists at her side. "And neither am I." Heat flooded her cheeks and tears burned in her eyes.

Strauth's expression softened. "I didn't mean—"

"To accuse me?" She wiped the tears from her face and shook her head. "My father is not a murderer. My family does not condone the things Morzaun has done."

Strauth took a few steps forward, the fire returning to the darkening look in his eyes. "Your father helped Morzaun kill General Fyord and the princess, not to mention he made an attempt on King Sytal's life."

"What? That isn't true!"

He stepped closer. "They entered the palace that night hoping to kidnap Morzaun's son, and when my father tried to stop them, they murdered him in cold blood! He died trying to protect Princess Senniva from Morzaun, her own husband. And then they went for our king, but the army of Izarden showed up before they could finish their schemes."

"Stop."

"Your father is responsible for the deaths—"

"Stop!"

He was so close, she could feel his heat. His chest rose and fell with heavy breaths, just like hers. His voice had never sounded so cold. "The truth is drenched with blood and your father is at the center of it—painful as it may be for you to hear."

"It seems you know nothing of the truth, Lieutenant." He opened his mouth to rebuff, but she slipped past him. "Whoever told you those details—lied. That is *not* what happened."

"And I'm supposed to just take your word for it? Your statements accuse our former king of deceit. That's blasphemy against the throne of Izarden."

"I don't care! King Sytal was rather good at lying"—she looked him over with a deep scowl—"clearly. He has everyone thoroughly convinced he was innocent, and I will not stand here defending myself against you. Not when your mind is so clearly made on the matter.

"Good. No need to bother when I could never believe the word of a *witch*."

He winced the moment the word left his mouth. Her lip quivered, and she wrapped her arms around herself. Why did his insults hurt so badly?

"Feya, I..."

He reached for her, and she stepped backwards to escape him. Regret filled his eyes again, but she would not be fooled by them anymore. "Unless you desire to know what really happened, there is no reason for you to speak to me again...*ever.*"

He frowned, causing his face to wrinkle. Feya spun around and dove onto her bed. She curled up beneath the covers, the only place she could hide before sobs overtook her composure. She waited several minutes for the sound of Strauth's boots clicking against the floor and the soft thud of the door.

The lieutenant's understanding of what had happened contained thin truths with deep lies. Someone had reconstructed the details, and those changes fueled a hatred Feya couldn't blame him for having. If everyone in Izarden believed such falsehoods, magic would never be accepted. King Sytal had twisted the truth to suit his own needs, and her family would pay the price for his deception.

CHAPTER ELEVEN
An Assassin in the Night

Light taps on his window only made Strauth's skin burn more as he paced across his room. If that bird wished to see another day, it had better stop pecking at the paned glass. He growled, making his forty-seventh retreat to his chamber door and spinning around again.

Things had been going perfectly. Strauth had managed three days without speaking to Feya. He didn't need the complications that came from talking to her, nor the feelings—ones he couldn't quite understand. He hated magic, yet she always seemed to find a way over his walls, and every time he slipped into a conversation with her, he forgot about his plan. Strauth couldn't afford to forget. He needed to be ready the moment Ivrin set things into motion.

And so, he had decided to ignore the witch.

Strauth winced. He hadn't meant to call her that out loud again, not because it wasn't true, but because he realized how much it hurt her. But why should he care? After all, he intended to take part in a scheme to kill those who wielded magic, and that included Feya.

His stomach twisted. The thought of ending her life bothered him. She seemed so innocent—so terrified of her own abilities. He had no doubt her desire to keep her magic from harming anyone was genuine, but that didn't mean she wasn't a threat.

Strauth had entered her chamber this morning bent on keeping to his plan. He'd placed her tray on the desk and then waited. Every time he served her meals or retrieved her empty trays, she met his gaze and offered him a smile. Though each one had made his chest constrict with guilt, he'd grown accustomed to seeing it, and admittedly, looked forward to the way even the smallest lift of her lips lit up her eyes.

But this morning she hadn't shared her smile with him. He had immediately panicked that something was wrong, a completely ridiculous over reaction. What did he expect? Her to keep smiling at him when he rewarded her attempts at politeness with a sour disposition? He couldn't blame her for giving up on her efforts, but Strauth already missed them.

"Confound it," he muttered. What was the matter with him?

He shook his head and paced towards his window, only to spin on his heels when the pesky red-winged creature flapped against the glass.

Unable to fight his desire for answers any longer, Strauth had finally asked Feya about her magic. He'd thought on little else the last few days, but one couldn't ask questions and ignore someone at the same time. The dilemma had eaten away at him until he'd lost all resolve—that, and the sadness in her eyes when she spoke of her loneliness matched a deep pain in his own soul. He understood all too well what it felt like.

Though she had answered his question, the conversation had dove into a dark abyss of anger and resentment. He'd unintentionally accused her of being a murderer, of being the one thing that she feared the most. Strauth regretted letting his temper get the better of him, but her words had sprouted his irritation. She'd claimed the details of what happened the night his father died were inaccurate.

Strauth could remember that day so clearly. He could still picture Ivrin's solemn expression when he sat with him and his mother to relay the news. Morzaun and Aldeth, two warlocks who possessed dark magic, had forced their way into the palace with the aim of kidnapping Morzaun's son. The sorcerer had once been married to the princess, but she had disowned their relationship when the man made threats against Izarden. Sytal had banished Morzaun and his fellow magic wielders, and the princess, who was pregnant at the time, had chosen to remain with her brother.

Eight years later, Morzaun took his revenge. He entered the palace and sought his wife. Strauth's father, the then general of Izarden, had tried to protect her. Both of them had lost their lives to magic that night. Morzaun and Aldeth hadn't stopped there, either.

They had intended to kill King Sytal as well, but were unable to complete the task. Many good men died that day in defense of their king.

Feya's words rang through his thoughts. She'd claimed his version of the details was flawed. Surely she was lying to protect her father? Yet he couldn't bring himself to believe that was true. The pain in her expression from his accusations had filled him with doubt. What if there was more to the events than he knew—than Ivrin knew? What would that mean for their plan?

He only wanted to eradicate magic because he believed those who wielded it were a threat, but if Aldeth and his family were innocent of any crimes, then that made Strauth no better than Morzaun. The man had wiped out half of Izarden's army and countless innocents with no thought of remorse. Hadn't he?

Strauth ran his fingers through his hair. He didn't know what to believe. Ivrin had told him to be careful around Feya. Was she just getting inside his head? Truthfully, she had since the moment he saw her.

The pecking across the room intensified, and he turned to face the offending sound. Two birds now flapped against his window. What the devil was wrong with them? Could he not be allowed to think in peace?

He'd just decided to open his window and give them a piece of his mind when a knock sounded at the door. Strauth parted the wood from the frame to find a young guard standing as stiff as a board before him. "Lieutenant," he said, giving him a firm salute. "Forgive the intrusion, but I thought you should be informed.

We've had a perimeter breach. Someone broke through about fifteen minutes ago. We don't know what they're after, but the guard who spotted them said they were armed."

A sudden urge to check on his ward made it difficult for Strauth to fill his lungs. "Where was the intruder last seen?"

"In the courtyard, sir. We've not been able to track their current whereabouts."

Strauth gave the man a nod and slipped past him. "I'll be in the"—he stopped himself before the word *witch* could pass over his lips—"our guest's chamber. Please keep me informed of the situation."

"Yes, sir."

Strauth dashed down the hall to Feya's room. He threw open the door, looking over his shoulder into the now empty corridor as he stepped inside. "Feya, there's—"

Strauth ducked, barely catching the light glistening off of the blade that swung towards him, and the dagger carved a long gash into the door. He stood, and another swing forced his back against the door, snapping it closed. Strauth dodged and maneuvered away from the weapon, but the person in tight black clothing and half mask pursued. He brandished his sword from his belt just in time to stop their dagger from meeting his face. Strauth grabbed their wrist, staring briefly into a set of emerald eyes before twisting his body and tossing the assailant over his shoulder. They landed on the ground with a thud and a groan.

Feya.

Strauth searched the room for her. She stood in the corner, trembling against the wall, completely panic-stricken. Her gaze met his. He needed to get her out of here.

He hadn't made it far when something heavy crashed against his head. The room spun and his body hit the floor. Pain pulsed along the back of his head and down his neck. He rubbed his fingers through his hair and a warm liquid coated them.

"No, please!" Feya shouted.

The assailant marched towards her, dagger in hand. Strauth jumped to his feet and stumbled to keep his balance. He gripped the assassin by the shoulder, and with as much strength as he could muster, threw them backwards.

A feminine voice grunted. She staggered, but remained upright. She?

Yes, the assassin was a woman. Her black hair wove in small, tight braids against her head and then cascaded over her shoulders, transitioning to a dark crimson at the ends. Besides the black mask covering half of her face, several lines of red scars curved across her cheeks, one trailing past the bridge of her nose.

Strauth positioned himself in front of Feya, holding his weapon at the ready. The assassin moved closer.

"I'd reconsider this if I were you," said Strauth.

"I'm only here for the girl. Move aside." She took another step, and Strauth fell back a pace. Warmth seeped into his shirt sleeve where Feya's petite fingers slid over his arm. She peeked around his shoulder, and the assassin laughed. "Are you truly willing to risk your life for a witch?"

Feya balled his clothes in her hand and stared up at him with pleading eyes. Did she still believe he wouldn't protect her? The thought sent an unseen dagger into his heart. He didn't want her to harbor such doubts about his character, but wasn't she right to do so?

"I'm more than willing," said Strauth, facing the assassin with new resolve. "I'd suggest you get out of here while you still can."

"Your funeral. Not mine."

The assassin lunged, and Strauth pressed Feya back, settling her against the wall. Loud clanks filled the chamber as they dueled. He shoved her and advanced, swinging his long sword. The woman dodged his attack and circled to his side. He raised his blade, following her movement. The lines near her eyes crinkled, her mask hiding a smirk.

Strauth had trained in Izarden's army for years and recognized skill. This woman had experience.

He shot towards her again, his blade sailing for her head. Ducking, she pivoted, and in a heartbeat, sprung forward. Her blade slid across his upper arm, slicing through his shirt.

Strauth screamed as pain shot to his fingertips. He grabbed his arm and stumbled back. Feya gasped as the assassin lunged. She flung herself in front of Strauth. What was she doing!

Strauth grabbed her around the waist, and spun them both out of the assassin's path. The tip of her blade stuck into the window frame, the wood cracking as it sank in. Strauth regained his footing just as the assassin yanked her dagger free.

"Strauth!" Feya yelled as the assassin advanced.

He tossed Feya out of the assailant's reach and swatted her dagger away with his sword before throwing a punch at her jaw. The woman evaded, but not quickly enough to avoid him completely. His fist smacked into her shoulder and a distinct *pop* met his ears. The assassin groaned, applying pressure to her dislocated arm as she withdrew from him. With a hard push on the appendage, it snapped back into place, and she screamed.

"You'll regret that," she spat, panting.

Strauth smirked. "I regret a lot of things; that won't be one of them."

The assassin raced forward and rammed into Strauth, tackling him to the ground. They both struggled to get the upper hand, their weapons entangling and ripping at each other's flesh.

The assassin elbowed him in the face and smacked his arm down. His sword clattered against the floor. Strauth grabbed the woman's wrist before she could plunge her blade into his chest. She hissed, and with her free hand, ripped another dagger from her belt and swiped it across his thigh. A stream of pain shot down his leg before she stabbed her blade into his abdomen. Strauth stiffened, his whole body pulsing in agony. He gasped, and the assassin pushed forward, forcing him the rest of the way to the floor. Her lips curled as he hit the ground, and she dug the blade in deeper. Blood filled his mouth, blocking his scream. He gripped her wrist and attempted to pull the piece out of his stomach, but the pain paralyzed his muscles. The woman lifted her hand, ready to plunge the second dagger into his heart.

He barely glimpsed the blur of movement in the corner of his eye. Feya barreled into the assassin, and the contact ripped the blade from his body. He gasped and the room spun. Vague, muffled voices grew louder. The assassin staggered to her feet, and her widening eyes shot to the door and then to Feya. She cursed before bolting for the entry, throwing it open and disappearing into the hall. Loud shouts ensued, followed by guards rushing past.

Feya crouched next to him, her voice frantic as she looked him over. "No, no, no..."

Strauth pressed his hand to the open wound in his stomach, the action igniting pain through his body and blurring his vision. Blood oozed between his fingers as he struggled to breathe.

Feya covered his hand, adding more pressure, and he yelped, causing blood to splatter from his mouth. Her face pinched, and tears streamed down her cheeks. Strauth's eyes fluttered closed as a metallic taste continuously washed over his tongue. He'd fought to stay alert, and not give in to the pressing darkness that threatened to overtake him. Warmth on his cheek drew his eyes open. Feya had placed her other hand there, and the tenderness with which she held him sent a strange sensation through him.

"Stay with me," she whispered, choking on the words. "Please, stay with me."

Her plea struck his soul. He couldn't understand why his current state would affect her—not when he'd done little to deserve it—but her reaction soothed a deep ache inside him, a longing he hadn't realized existed.

He lifted his hand to cover hers and leaned into her touch. The pressing darkness encroached upon him, filling his vision. He wouldn't survive this, but at least she was safe. He would die knowing he'd proven his character to her, and somehow that knowledge was enough to give him peace.

Strauth took one last shuddering breath, and the world faded into shadows.

CHAPTER TWELVE
A Gift of Magic

Strauth's hand fell from hers and his eyes closed. Feya patted his face, hoping it would bring that stormy blue gaze back to her, but he remained unresponsive. Her heart hammered. She couldn't lose him, not when he'd risked his life to protect her.

"Strauth!" she shouted, placing both hands over his heart. The soft thuds were barely detectable. He was alive, but only just. Blood drenched his military uniform from his gut, arm, and thigh.

"He's losing too much blood," she whispered, moving her hands over his wound. Her fingers instantly turned red. "I have to heal him. I have to..." She choked on a sob, a sense of dire doubt filling her chest. She hadn't successfully performed a spell in nearly a year, and now a life hung on whether she could overcome her inability. What if she couldn't?

She shook her head and drew a deep breath. She had to try.

Feya recited the words to the healing spell. They slipped from her lips with ease, but no purple light appeared to accompany them. She tried again, and the results remained the same. Sobs interrupted the incantation as she continued into a third attempt. For so long, Feya had been afraid to use her magic, and she hadn't been sad when her ability to use her power had faded.

But now, she desperately wanted it back.

Without it, Strauth would die, and the fault would rest on her shoulders. How could she live with such a thing?

Feya leaned forward and brushed his hair from his forehead. "I'm so sorry."

She trailed her fingers along his jaw. The last few days, he'd made it clear that he hated her. Yet in that moment, when his eyes had met hers for the last time and he'd leaned into her touch, his expression had told a different story.

No. She wouldn't just give up. Strauth had to live. She needed to understand the strange connection between them.

Feya placed her hands on his stomach and began chanting the incantation again. She kept her eyes closed and gave all of her energy and focus to the spell. Warmth spread through her body, flowing like fire through her veins. When the last syllable passed her lips, she opened her eyes just in time to glimpse her purple aura dissipating from around her hands.

She held her breath, and silence seized the room. She could hear muffled shouts beyond her window as the guards continued their search for the assassin, but none of that mattered now.

Strauth's body convulsed, and his sharp gasp startled her. He bolted upright, coughing. His gaze darted around the room until it landed on her. Feya beamed when his brows pinched. She'd done it. She'd saved him!

Her body trembled, and she struggled for breath as though she'd just run across the entire width of Verascene. She resisted the urge to throw her arms around the lieutenant's neck. Strauth pressed his bloodied fingers into his abdomen, as if completely confused.

"You... healed me?" he muttered, his eyes going wide with the realization.

Shouts echoed from outside the palace, and Strauth didn't give her time to respond. He jumped to his feet and grabbed her by the wrist. The lieutenant pulled her up and led her out into the corridor with a haste that did nothing to ease her heaving chest. Being too stunned by the evening's events, she followed without hesitation.

Halfway down the hall, Strauth threw open the door to another chamber and guided her inside towards the bed. With no lanterns to illuminate the area, shadows shrouded everything in the room. Only the small trickle of moonlight provided any visibility, but from what she could tell, this chamber wasn't currently in use.

"Get down on the floor and stay by the bed," he said. It was an order, but his tone was so gentle that she almost thought she'd imagined it. Regardless, her body seemed incapable of moving on its own. Strauth released his hand from her wrist and placed it higher on her arm, startling her. "Feya, please get down on the ground. Stay here until I get back."

"You're leaving?"

"Yes."

He turned and started for the door. Panic seized her, and Feya latched onto his arm, bringing him to a stop and capturing his attention. "She almost killed you! *Please*, stay with me. Don't go."

His eyes searched hers, as if contemplating her request. Strauth brushed a strand of hair from her face, sweeping it behind her ear, and the soft brush of his fingers sent a wave of chills rippling through her. "I promise I'll be right back, but I need you to keep hidden until I find out what happened—until I know the assassin is no longer a threat."

She released her hold and nodded. What was the matter with her? She was being completely irrational. This man hated her. Why, then, did she feel like her world would crumble if something happened to him? "Be careful and don't forget you promised to come back."

His lips curled, and a hint of mischief danced in his eyes. "I must offer a somewhat decent view for you to be so insistent."

She laughed and then reined in the sound, giving him a pointed look that curled his lips even more. Strauth didn't smile often, at least not around her, and that was probably a good thing the way it twisted her insides.

"Just hurry back," she said, kneeling on the floor and leaning against the bed.

He nodded and stepped out into the corridor, shutting the door behind him. Feya squeezed her knees against her chest, fighting the tears forming in her eyes.. She focused on her breathing and the exercise calmed her.

She'd performed a spell.

Feya held her hands in front of her. It had been so long since she'd used magic, and she hadn't realized how much she missed the warm sensation that spread through her. She didn't regret saving Strauth in the slightest.

Her joy melted into fear and she frowned. What if by doing so she had opened the doors for darkness to pry its way into her heart? It was the only explanation for what had happened to her uncle, Morzaun. Magic had changed him, made him do things he wouldn't have otherwise.

She analyzed her hands further, taking in the streaks of crimson that tainted her skin. Strauth's blood was everywhere: on her hands, her arms, her dress...she wouldn't have been surprised if red splotches also covered her face.

The minutes dragged on, and the steady hoot of an owl replaced the muffled voices of the guards outside. After what felt like an eternity, footsteps echoed outside in the hall. The chamber door flew open and smashed against the wall. Days ago, such a thing would have made her jump, but the noise was oddly soothing. Only her lieutenant entered the room like that.

Strauth's boots clicked against the floor with what sounded like a hasty stride. He crouched in front of her, his stoic expression revealing nothing. How did he stay so composed after everything that had happened?

"Did they catch her?" she asked.

He heaved a sigh. "She slipped past them. They chased her to the edge of the city and then lost track of her in the shadows of the forest."

Feya swallowed hard against the lump in her throat. How would she ever feel safe again knowing an assassin had been hired to kill her? "What if she comes back?"

"I've increased the patrol, but she'd be a fool to come back tonight."

Tonight. How reassuring. What about tomorrow or the next day? How long would she have to live in terror?

Her fear must have shown on her face, because Strauth's brows pinched with concern. "I'll keep you safe, Feya. I give you my word." His face contorted, and he averted his gaze. Did he regret making her such a promise? Whether he did or didn't, she believed him. Everything inside her said he would protect her, even if he hated magic. He'd certainly proved that tonight.

Feya still had a hard time believing she'd actually accessed her power. She'd brought him back from the brink of death, but had she completely healed him? He seemed healed—no expression of pain lingering in his features—but his blood-soaked clothes filled her with doubt.

"Are you all right?" she whispered.

Strauth's eyes met hers, and for a moment he didn't answer. "I'm fine, thanks to you."

"I'm glad. I thought..." Her throat constricted, keeping the words from finding their way out of her mouth.

He wrapped his hand around hers, and she instinctively curled her fingers to keep it in place. His gentle squeeze of her hand comforted Feya in ways she couldn't describe. His voice settled over her with softness, but not without question. "You told me you couldn't use your magic?"

"I didn't think I could, but you were dying, and I..." Her tears broke free. "I just kept trying and trying. I didn't think it would work. There was so much blood, and you were so pale, and—"

"Feya." His hand cupped her cheek, and her breath hitched. "It's all right. I believe you. Thank you for not giving up on me." His thumb brushed across her skin, removing her tears—or maybe blood. Was she even still crying? She wasn't sure anymore. His touch had muddled her ability to think clearly.

He dropped his hand, and part of her saddened at the absence of his warmth. "We should get you cleaned up." He glanced at his hands and clothes. "Both of us."

Strauth slid his hands around her waist and under her knees. He lifted her to the bed, and before she could protest, set her down. "I'll be back in just a minute," he said. She nodded and watched him disappear into the corridor.

He returned with a bowl of water, several rags, and a small lantern. The lieutenant drew the curtains closed and then sat down beside her. Strauth wrung the water from one of the cloths and handed it to her, his eyes sweeping over what she guessed were blotches of red on her face before he proceeded to take care of his own. Feya started with her cheeks, keeping her gaze forward as she scrubbed.

Images of Strauth lying on her chamber floor with a dagger protruding from his stomach forced their way into her mind. She looked at her hands, and the sight of red made her scour over her skin, desperate to rid herself of the reminders of the night's events. The tainted cloth shook in her fingertips, and she scrubbed her wrist so hard it burned.

"Feya, stop."

She ignored him. She needed to get it off—needed to forget.

Strauth's hands fell over hers. He tugged at the blood-stained linen, and she allowed it to slip from her fingers. She held in a sob. He would think her weak if she let it escape. She'd already released enough tears.

"Feya, it's all right if you cry. I won't judge you for it."

The sincerity in his eyes made her lip quiver. Strauth rinsed her cloth but didn't give it back. Instead, his hand hovered next to her cheek. "May I help?"

"Please," she said, choking on the word.

For the next several minutes, he wiped away whatever blood remained on her face and hands. His touch was gentle, just as it had been the day he'd tended to her wounds after she'd tried to escape, and the care he took in cleaning her skin left her breathless. He returned the rag to the water once he'd finished.

Strauth's gaze fell to the stains on her dress. The new streaks of red, which had joined the spot from when she'd injured herself trying to escape, had already dried, leaving the fabric stiff and hard.

"Tomorrow I'll see to getting you new clothes. For now, try to get some rest. It's been a long night."

She couldn't argue with that, but the idea of closing her eyes when there was still an assassin out there who wanted her dead twisted her stomach. Feya couldn't imagine she'd actually be able to sleep under the circumstances. Not tonight—maybe never.

"What if—"

"She's not going to come back. You're safe."

He stared at her for a long moment, and an image of him wrapping her in his arms sent her heart into a frantic rhythm. Blue skies over Virgamor, what was wrong with her?

His gaze dropped, lingering briefly on her lips, and she went rigid.

Strauth stood, shaking his head as though frustrated, but about what, she didn't know. "Try to get some sleep. If you need anything, I'm in the room next door."

"How am I to do that with the door locked?"

His lips twitched, and she was suddenly very aware of how his beard framed them perfectly.

"You promised me you wouldn't try to escape again, and I think I trust you enough to leave it unlocked."

"I suppose saving your life has its benefits then."

Strauth chuckled, but quickly covered his amusement by clearing his throat. "Possibly." He drummed his fingers against his leg, restoring his impassive expression. "I bid you goodnight, then. Try to rest, and let me know if you need anything."

What she needed was peace of mind. Unfortunately, the lieutenant was unknowingly taking that with him. She felt safer with him in the room, but she would be strong. The last thing the man would want to do after nearly dying is sit with her all night.

"Goodnight, Strauth."

He gave her one last look over his shoulder, and whether he meant to offer her a smile or not, one found its way onto his face. Her heart dropped into her stomach. Perhaps he didn't hate her after all.

CHAPTER THIRTEEN
The Art of Pretending

Strauth was too tired to be pacing his room, but he couldn't seem to stop himself. He hadn't slept a wink last night, and not just because he'd fought off an assassin and returned from the edges of death. He should have tried to sleep, but after changing his clothes, had found himself incapable of being anywhere but sitting outside Feya's door until the sun had risen to chase away the shadows. The assassin would have been foolish to return, yet he still couldn't leave her. He'd even peeked inside several times to make sure she was all right.

Not that she could be after almost being assassinated.

Her quiet sobs had pulled at him, and his desire to comfort her had almost led him to her bedside. Strauth told himself it was only because she had saved his life, but denying the truth proved a wasted endeavor.

The woman he'd been assigned to guard continued to fill his thoughts more and more with each passing day, and he could no longer put on a façade of hatred. She'd slowly eaten away at his resolve, and now he wondered if he had misplaced his anger from the start. Were the details he possessed about his father's death misguided?

Of course, this was only the least of his problems. He needed to get to the bottom of the events leading up to King Sytal's death, but there were other matters to attend to as well—namely, his increasing attraction to the woman. Last night, after they'd spent half an hour cleaning his blood off their skin, he'd imagined kissing her.

It wasn't as though Strauth had never kissed a woman before, but the desire had never overcome him so thoroughly as it had after Feya saved his life and expressed concern for his safety. In fact, many of the feelings she elicited from him he'd never experienced. Given that he and Ivrin were planning to put an end to magic, this problem of his didn't exactly bode well.

"I need to find out the truth," he muttered, making another lap between his chamber walls. "If Aldeth and his family are innocent, then we have to stop this scheme. I won't end innocent lives, even if they are a potential threat to Izarden."

Taps on his window pulled him to a halt in the center of the room. The two winged nuisances had returned.

"The devil take it," he said with a growl and marched to the window. "I'm putting an end to *them* right now."

Strauth pushed open the glass, and the two frantically flapping birds flew into his chamber. He swatted at them with his sword as they sailed around the room. This ridiculous situation was doing nothing but adding to his fatigue. Breathing heavily, Strauth sheathed his blade. Without the chaos of his swinging weapon, the birds landed on his desk. It was only then that he noticed that they both held rolls of parchment in their talons.

What in Virgamor?

He approached them slowly, hoping they wouldn't take flight again, and to his surprise, they dropped their parcels. Strauth picked up the first and unrolled it.

> *Strauth,*
>
> *I've ordered Aldeth to use his magic to have this delivered more quickly than sending a messenger. During our travels to Rowenport, I have successfully found an assassin for hire. She has agreed to help put our plan into motion with proper payment. I will send you more details tomorrow. Until then, send a response so I know you've received this correspondence.*
>
> *Ivrin*

Strauth's stomach dropped. Ivrin had hired the assassin. He

reached for the second parchment so abruptly that he startled the birds, and they both flew back out his window.

Strauth,

Did you receive my first letter? The attack will take place two nights hence. You needn't be involved other than to stay out of her way when she executes her services. Keep the witch's death hushed until Aldeth has fulfilled his end of the king's agreement. Then we will finish the rest of them.

Ivrin

His heart raced. Ivrin was sure to be angry when he found out Strauth had done the exact opposite. He'd defended Feya, although his efforts hadn't been the most satisfactory. He'd failed to protect her and nearly lost his life in the process. Feya had healed him—saved him—and he still didn't understand why. Strauth hadn't been kind to her, and yet she had wept over his injured body. She had begged him not to leave her.

His chest constricted. Feya cared about him, and though he had fought against it for days, he cared about her too. He needed to talk to Ivrin. Strauth didn't know if Aldeth was truly innocent, but Feya was, and he could no longer take part in a plan that would end in her death.

He closed his chamber window, and for several minutes, watched the sunrise illuminate the palace courtyard. Soon he would take

Feya her morning meal, but before he did that, there was one more thing he needed to attend to. Strauth pulled on his black coat and made his way to the door. He would write Ivrin a letter, requesting their plan be put on hold, and then he would visit a young lady that deserved his gratitude.

* * *

Strauth restrained a growl and drummed his fingers against his thigh. The woman before him planted her hands on her hips, her bushy grey eyebrows lifting high onto her forehead. What in Virgamor did she expect from him? How was he to know Feya's waist measurements or whether she preferred fitted sleeves to loose ones? Perhaps purchasing her a new dress hadn't been a wise decision.

"You need to give me at least a rough estimate, Lieutenant," the shopkeeper said with a high-pitched voice that made his ears ring. "You do realize women come in many shapes and sizes, don't you?"

"Yes, I'm quite aware, but that isn't something I pay much heed to. I don't go about measuring them on a regular basis."

"Nor buying them clothing, I'd wager," she muttered, and Strauth scowled. "Fine then. Describe her as best you can, and we'll have to hope for the best."

"She has long blonde hair, blue eyes—"

The woman whacked him on the shoulder. "What does the color of her hair and eyes have anything to do with her waist size or height? Honestly..." Her voice trailed off into something inaudible, but her expression suggested she was abundantly annoyed with him.

Strauth heaved a sigh. "All right, she's about this tall, and her waist"—he used his hands to demonstrate Feya's size—"is about like this."

The woman lifted one of her brows, eyeing him curiously before pulling out a dress and holding it in front of herself. "Does this look as though it will do? It would be much easier if you brought the young lady to see me."

"I can't bring her, and no, that one won't suit her. It's too broad in the shoulders. She's quite petite...and if you have something purple, I think that might work better than green."

The woman's lips curled and the look she passed him made heat crawl up the back of his neck. "You're quite right, Lieutenant. You haven't paid nearly enough heed to her figure."

She fumbled through a pile of fabric, and Strauth ignored the smug expression she displayed. She held up another dress, and Strauth took in its details. The dress was a soft lavender with grey cuffs and a long silver sash. He imagined what Feya would look like in such an elegant design.

Yes. This one would do just fine.

"I suppose that will work."

The woman wrapped the piece in a swatch of white linen. "I trust you know best, Lieutenant. After all, you seem to have already envisioned her wearing it."

More heat flooded his face. Had he been *that* obvious?

Strauth paid the woman and made his way back to the palace, vowing to never shop for women's clothing again, especially from shopkeepers who seemed able to read him too well. He unwrapped the cloth just enough to place this morning's other purchase inside—an ivory comb with intricately carved flowers in the center and a set of bristles on either side. He'd often seen Feya running her fingers through her hair and thought this might provide a welcomed relief from the task.

He entered the palace and headed for the guest wing, but before he could round the corner, a voice called after him. "Lieutenant!"

Strauth froze. That voice belonged to Ivrin.

The man stormed towards him with a scowl. "What's all this?" he asked, gesturing to the parcel in Strauth's hand.

"It's just...nothing important. What are you doing here? Where are Aldeth and his family? Have you caught Morzaun?"

The lines on Ivrin's forehead deepened. "There's been a bit of a complication on that front, but that doesn't matter right now. Why did you stop last night's...happenings? I told you to just stay out of the way."

"I didn't get your letters until this morning."

"What does that matter? Why would you defend the witch, anyway?" Strauth's stomach curled at the disdain that laced his brother's voice. "You had the opportunity to be rid of her, and what do you do instead? Save her!"

"Delran assigned me as her guard. What was I supposed to do?"

Ivrin glanced down the corridor as several servants went about their cleaning routine. He threw open the door to one of the rooms and pushed Strauth inside. "You're supposed to let her die." he answered once the door connected with the frame.

"We need to reconsider this plan. I don't think Feya is anything like Morzaun. She's innocent, and she saved my life last night."

Ivrin pushed Strauth's chest, pressing him against the wall. Heat filled his body, and Strauth restrained the urge to shove his brother back. Ivrin held his finger in front of Strauth's face. "She wouldn't have needed to save you if you'd stayed out of the way. Now the assassin is asking double to make a second attempt. You are to blame for this, and it will come out of your pockets—not mine. Two thousand gold pieces, Strauth. That is what you will owe the assassin."

"That's everything I have! Everything Father left me."

"Perhaps you should have considered that when you saved that *witch*. Had you not intervened, we'd have one less problem to deal with."

Ivrin reached into his pocket and brandished a piece of parchment from inside. He thrust it into Strauth's hands. "Instructions. I'd suggest you follow them this time. Assassins don't take kindly to not being paid."

"But I—"

"You *will* pay her, Strauth! That's an order!" Ivrin backed away, his eyes dark. "And you will spend the next few years paying me back for your incompetence. I'd suggest you don't disappoint me again."

He wanted nothing more than to argue with Ivrin, but the man wasn't just his brother. He was the general, and Strauth was duty bound to follow his orders.

Ivrin straightened his coat, his frown firmly in place. "Fetch the girl. The king requires her in the Great Hall while he has a *discussion* with Aldeth."

Strauth's eyes widened. "A discussion about what?"

"Just do as you're told, Strauth. Bring the girl. And when I give you a nod, make sure Aldeth knows what any act of treason will mean for his daughter. Convince him...or better yet, convince *me*. Prove to me you're not as worthless as I think you are."

Strauth winced. At one time, Ivrin's approval had been all he wanted, but he wasn't so sure anymore. "I'll go get her."

"Good. See to it that you don't mess this up, Strauth. We can't afford mistakes, especially not with Delran watching." Ivrin yanked open the door and stormed away. Going against his brother's wishes wasn't an option, but perhaps he could find a way around them that allowed him to follow orders and keep Feya safe. Strauth took a deep breath and walked to her room. He'd have to sort it out later.

Feya stood by the window when he entered, and she offered him a smile the moment she turned around. "Good morning, Strauth," she said, moving towards him.

"How are you? Did you sleep?"

She shook her head. He'd suspected not, and he could hardly blame her.

"I'm afraid breakfast will have to wait, but I did come bearing a gift." He offered her the linen-wrapped parcel.

Feya's brows bunched. "What's this?"

"Generally, one must open a gift to find that out," he answered, slipping it into her hands. The brush of his skin against hers tied knots in his stomach.

Feya eyed him with mock suspicion before turning her attention to the cloth. She gaped as layers of fabric spilled to the ground and she held the ivory comb near her face. "These are beautiful! You brought these for me?"

"You saved my life. It was the least I could do, and besides, my blood has clearly ruined your dress."

"Yes, I suppose it has. And the comb? Is that because you find my appearance so displeasing?"

"What? No. I haven't given your appearance any thought—I mean, I have...obviously. But not like—I just noticed your hair was...not that I care what it looks like. I knew you didn't have one—a comb—and you're always using your fingers, so I thought it would help. Not that I think your appearance needs help. I..." He snapped his mouth closed.

Confound it.

Feya turned away, giggling, and his face burned. He'd never been the sort to become flustered, but today was proving him more than capable of the experience. Strauth cleared his throat. "You should change. I'm supposed to take you to see the king."

She turned to face him again. "Thank you for the gifts, Strauth."

His finger tapped against his leg, the only thing he could do to keep himself from pacing. "You're welcome."

For several moments, they stared at each other.

Feya dropped her gaze. "I suppose I should change."

When he didn't respond, she bit her lip—lips he was now struggling to not give any attention. "If I'm not mistaken, Lieutenant, I believe you said I had nothing to entice you to watch. Unless you've changed your mind?"

Virgamor. She was waiting for him to leave.

Strauth spun around. He should have left the room, but his legs seemed to have forgotten how to walk. He heard a low chuckle and then the rustle of fabric. His heart pounded, and he chided his eyes for wandering to his shoulder.

"All right," she said, after several minutes of awkward silence. "Do I look a bit more presentable?"

He turned around and swallowed. Presentable would have been an understatement, but confessing as much would only fluster him more.

"It suits you," he mumbled.

Her cheeks colored. "My lieutenant has excellent tastes."

My lieutenant? His heart might explode. "I know nothing about having excellent tastes, but I'm glad you approve." He gestured towards the door. "We should probably get going. The king will be waiting." And he needed to get out of this room before he made himself look more foolish than he already had.

Feya walked beside him towards the Great Hall, and when they neared the stone archway and the guards, Strauth wrapped his fingers around her arm.

Appearances. An act. Not so long ago, he'd accused Aldeth of being the performer, but today it was his turn. The thought made him nauseous.

Feya's father stood before Delran, and the moment she saw him, she tried to jerk out of his hold. As much as he wanted to allow her to go to him, he couldn't.

"Papa!"

Aldeth turned, his brows pinched. "Feya."

He started to move, but a sword fell into his path, and Ivrin gave him a stern look. Strauth tugged Feya towards the king, keeping some distance between her and Aldeth.

"Am I to understand that you've betrayed Izarden?" asked Delran, his tone dark. "You allowed Morzaun to escape. What do you have to say about this, Aldeth?"

"My King, it was not my intention for him to allude us, but—"

"Your son made sure of that," said Ivrin, sneering. "Zeeran protected Morzaun the moment Aldeth launched a spell. He defended the sorcerer, and Aldeth refused to fight back. Morzaun escaped capture because of his unwillingness."

"He is my son!" shouted Aldeth. "I won't bring harm to my family solely to capture Morzaun."

Delran stood, his expression merciless. "Then I suppose you'll have to decide which member of your family you wish to protect."

Strauth met Ivrin's gaze, and his brother gave him a firm nod. He hesitated to move, and Ivrin's eyes shrank to pinpricks. He didn't have a choice. He had orders to follow, but that didn't mean he wouldn't do so begrudgingly. Strauth pulled Feya against him, wrapping one arm across her waist and pinning her arm at her side. The other pulled his sword from its sheath and held it to her throat. She gasped, and her free hand pried at his wrist, attempting to pull the blade away.

"No, please!" said Aldeth, taking a step towards them.

Strauth's heart plummeted into his stomach. He had no desire to do this, but it was better that he pretend than Ivrin or a guard hold Feya. At least he could protect her. Strauth moved the metal as close to her throat as he dared and put on a fierce expression. The performance stopped Aldeth in his tracks.

"Think carefully now, warlock," spat Delran. "Either you hold up your end of our deal and bring me Morzaun, or she meets an untimely death."

Feya sobbed, and the sound pained Strauth's soul. She wiggled against him, and he feared the blade might accidentally slice her skin. He tightened his hold, but she only squirmed more. Ivrin had instructed him to convince Aldeth...to convince *him*, but Feya didn't need to believe the act. Strauth dipped his chin next to her ear, whispering softly. "Feya, *please* stop moving. I don't want to hurt you."

She stopped, and her body relaxed. His heart gave a happy lurch. She trusted him.

Strauth slid his hand subtly down her arm until it found hers, and he curled his fingers around it with a gentle squeeze. He stroked his thumb over her skin. Her breathing eased, and the sobs faded.

"I'll do what you ask," said Aldeth. "But, please, don't hurt my daughter. I beg of you."

Delran stroked his long beard. "So long as you do as you promised, she'll not be harmed."

No, she wouldn't. Strauth would make sure of that.

"You have my word," said Aldeth. "Please."

Delran returned to his throne, his smug expression making Strauth's insides twist. "Good. Take her back to her room. We've more to discuss that she need not be present for."

Gladly. He was done acting.

Strauth sheathed his sword and took Feya by the arm. "Wait!" she pleaded. "Please, let me say goodbye!"

He halted and turned to face the king. Delran swatted the air and scoffed. "Make it quick then."

Strauth released her arm, and Feya ran to Aldeth, who wrapped his daughter in a tight embrace. Ivrin poked the tip of his sword into the warlock's back, making him flinch. "Don't you dare try anything."

"Are you all right, sweetheart?" asked Aldeth, his voice quiet.

"That's long enough," Delran said with a growl.

Feya lifted onto her toes and whispered into her father's ear, but Strauth was close enough to hear her words. "I'm fine, Papa. I promise. The lieutenant has kept me safe."

Something akin to pride swelled in his chest, but it was quickly hewn down by the hard glare Aldeth fired in his direction. He caught one from Ivrin as well, who'd likely heard Feya's statement. Strauth's acting seemed to have convinced the warlock, if not his brother.

"Time to go," he said, taking her arm and hoping she could see through his façade of disdain. She followed without hesitation, but Strauth exaggerated his expression as he pretended to drag Feya into the corridor. The moment they were past the guards, he loosened his hold, guiding her by the elbow back to her room. Her body trembled, and he hated himself for the role he'd played in causing her distress. Would *she* hate him for it?

They entered her new room—the one next to his own—and Strauth closed the door. He turned to face her. "Feya, I'm so sorry. Did I hurt you?"

Her face wrinkled, and she shook her head.

He didn't know what else to say. All Strauth wanted to do was comfort her, but he didn't have the slightest clue how to do that. Before he could come to any conclusion on the matter, Feya darted forward and threw herself against him. His body went stiff when she wrapped her arms around his waist, and he instinctively lifted his to enfold her.

No one had ever held him that way, nor he them. No one had ever needed *him* like this.

Feya melted against his chest, the contact spreading heat through his body. Could she hear the frantic thuds beneath her ear?

Her shuddering inhale wreaked tremors through her, and only made him hold her tighter. Did she feel safe in his arms? She seemed to, judging by the way she had tucked herself against him.

And he intended to keep it that way. He *wanted* her to feel safe with him.

Strauth rested his chin on her head. So long as he lived, he wouldn't let any harm befall her. He would protect her, even from his own brother.

CHAPTER FOURTEEN
Dismantling the Lies

Feya rested her forehead against the paned glass, staring down into the courtyard. Her thoughts constantly raced with the worst scenarios—ones that always ended with her losing the people she loved most. She bit her lip and dropped her gaze to Papa's letter once more.

> *Dear Feya,*
>
> *I hope this letter finds you well. Your mother, Ladisias, and I continue our search for your uncle. Since Zeeran left us, tracking him has become more difficult. The general*

grows anxious, and often loses his patience. The man has become increasingly on edge the last few days, and I suspect something more than Morzaun alluding capture bothers him, though what, I cannot say. Do not worry over our safety. I've reminded General Ivrin—politely—of our abilities, and he continues to keep a cautious distance. Despite his arrogance, I believe even he knows an attack on us would be foolish.

I miss you terribly and worry after you, especially since my last meeting with Delran. I cannot tell you how desperately I wanted to remove you from the palace, but your mother assured me no harm would befall you. She's had a vision of us all returning to Verascene, and that has offered a bit of peace to my restless soul, but as you know, visions do not always come to pass. Our paths can always change, whether by our own choices or the choices of others. Your mother saw Zeeran return with us, but I fear that will not be the case.

Regardless, I find myself needing confirmation. I've sent a piece of blank parchment along with this letter. Return it so that I know you are well. Keep the letter hidden. It would not bode well for the general or lieutenant to learn of this correspondence.

All my love,

Papa

Feya tucked the letter under the cushions. She'd sent the parchment back, and although Papa had told her not to worry about them, she couldn't help herself. He'd said General Ivrin was anxious. She supposed Delran's expectation for him to locate Morzaun weighed on the man, but something in her gut told her it was more than that. The entire situation made her uneasy and seeing the assassin's emerald eyes in her sleep did nothing to help.

Had her nightmares been a vision? That she'd seen the assassin before even stepping foot inside the palace couldn't be coincidence. Feya had never had visions before. If only she could talk to Mama, perhaps she might sort them out.

The king's accusations rattled through her mind. Zeeran had betrayed them. Her brother had protected Morzaun. He'd always had a soft spot for their uncle and had struggled to place any blame on him for the things that had happened, but Feya never imagined he would turn his back on his family. What had pushed him over the edge?

It wasn't as though she could ask King Delran to explain. Did Strauth have more details? She suspected he might. It was only after her recent encounter with both him and the general present that she realized they looked similar. She had concluded they must be related—brothers, perhaps. If that was the case, Strauth would likely know more, but whether he would share with her was another thing entirely.

They had spoken little the last few days, and not for lack of his attempts. She hadn't meant to push him away, especially after he'd comforted her with such tenderness following her visit to the Great Hall, but she was struggling to come to terms with everything, on top of the conflicting emotions she experienced around the lieutenant.

Feya rolled the fabric of her dress between her fingers, and a smile stole across her face. She hadn't expected Strauth to purchase her a dress. When he'd said he would find her new clothes, she'd assumed the attire would comprise a plain brown frock, something simple like what the palace servants' wore, but he'd completely surprised her. The dress was beautiful, and the comb he'd gifted her was the most intricate she'd ever seen. Both would have claimed no small coin.

Perhaps he'd only wished to convey his gratitude for her saving his life, but the gesture meant more to her than he knew. An act of kindness, especially from someone who had seemed to so thoroughly despise her when she'd first arrived, meant the world to Feya.

Her chamber door crashed against the wall, and Feya's lips curled a little. They hadn't spoken much recently, but the lieutenant's presence still filled her with comfort. She lifted her head from the glass and watched him set her breakfast on the table—and his own—next to her full tray from last night.

Strauth's brows pinched, and he met her gaze. "Will you come have breakfast with me?"

She dipped her chin. "I'm not hungry."

"Feya, you need to eat something."

The concern in his voice ate at her composure. When had he begun to care about her well-being? The transition had occurred so seamlessly that she didn't even know when it had started. Perhaps she was only imagining it.

But she didn't imagine the warmth that flowed over her when he sat down on the bench, nor the strong arm that wrapped around her and pulled her gently against him. His fingers trailing up and down her arm weren't a figment of her imagination either, and the press of what she assumed was his lips to the top of her head confirmed this was more than a dream.

His breath rustled her hair. "Everything is going to be all right."

"Did Zeeran really betray us? Did he really protect my uncle?"

Strauth tightened his hold around her, and she focused on his scent, some mixture of leather and pine, to calm her breathing.

"Yes, I'm afraid so. They're tracking them both, but it is much more difficult now that your uncle has magic on his side again."

Feya sat up, pulling away enough to meet his eyes. "What will the king do to him? Will he punish him? Will he..."

She wasn't naïve. The king had spoken of giving Morzaun a trial, but she had doubted his punishment would be anything less than death. Would Zeeran face the same consequence?

Strauth brushed a strand of hair from her face, and she shuddered. "I don't know, Feya, but I imagine Zeeran will face charges for his actions. I won't speculate as to what those will be, but..."

He sighed and slid his fingers to her shoulder, where they played with her hair. Had she combed it this morning? She couldn't remember. She couldn't think well at all with him doing that.

"Zeeran has always struggled with the way people have treated us," she said. "The distrust. The banishment. I think he believes my uncle's actions were justified."

Strauth's face hardened, and her stomach twisted. Feya averted her gaze. The topic had been a sore spot between them, and the last thing she wanted was to evoke his anger again. She didn't want to lose the comfort he offered. She didn't want to be alone.

His fingers curled under her chin and lifted her head. "I want to know the truth. I'm ready to listen, to understand."

Feya gulped. She wanted to tell him everything, to correct all the details he had wrong, but would he believe her? She didn't want to risk losing him, but the sincerity in his expression coaxed the words out of her.

"Before King Ekkhard died, he told my uncle that he feared his son, Sytal, had a lust for power that his inheritance of the throne would not satisfy. The king asked him to do whatever he could—whatever was necessary—to protect Izarden. After Ekkhard passed, Sytal asked Morzaun—and my mother and father—to help him take over other kingdoms. The three of them refused, and because of that, Sytal exiled them."

"Sytal told the people that Morzaun desired to send us to war, not the other way around."

"I imagine he did. He wanted the people to hate those who wielded magic—hate those who possessed the greatest threat to his reign. My uncle agreed to leave Izarden, but Sytal wanted reassurance that he would not try to stop him, so he held Princess Senniva, my aunt, hostage."

Strauth tapped his fingers against his leg. "You're saying Princess

Senniva was held here against her will, that she didn't disown her husband? That's quite a different story than the one Sytal recounted to the people, Feya."

She could hear the doubt in his voice, and it scared her. There was so much to explain, but how much of it could she trust giving him? If Strauth was close to the general, he might pass along information. Feya needed to be careful. If there was one thing she couldn't reveal, it was where her family currently resided. No one knew where they had found a home, and she feared what Delran might do with that knowledge should he find out.

Strauth twisted a piece of her hair around his finger, and her heart stammered. "What happened next?"

"We left Izarden. Papa said it was difficult for my uncle to stay away from his wife and son, but they corresponded through letters. My father would use his abilities to have them delivered. Aunt Senniva would send him information about Sytal's plans, movements of Izarden's army... He and my father would occasionally intervene. They did what they could to keep Sytal from gaining more power.

"Eight years after we left, King Sytal discovered my cousin, Eramus—Morzaun's son—could wield magic. Aunt Senniva was terrified that her brother would force him to do his bidding, so she...she sent him away. One of her handmaidens took Eramus out of Izarden."

"Eramus is alive?"

His arm disappeared from around her shoulder.

"We're not certain whether he is alive. My mother saw them in a vision. They boarded a ship, and the vessel was lost in a storm. We don't know if he survived."

"I thought...we were told that your uncle killed his son out of some act of revenge. Right before he killed the princess."

The mountain of lies that Sytal had spewed disgusted her. How many more had he spread among the people just to cover his own sins and create hatred for those who used magic?

Strauth's breathing had grown heavy. She covered one of his hands with her own, and his expression softened. "My uncle did not kill his wife or his son. He loved them both—dearly. When Sytal found out what his sister had done, he killed her. She refused to tell him where she'd sent Eramus, and he murdered her. My mother saw it unfold in a vision. She told Morzaun, and he and my father went to Izarden. They were hoping to save her before..."

Feya had been only nine when the devastating event occurred, but the details still pained her heart. One man's lust for power had ruined so many lives.

"They didn't come to the palace intending to kill anyone?" asked Strauth.

"No, they only wanted to save her. But they were too late. By the time they arrived in Izarden, Sytal had already killed Senniva. General Fyord told them—"

"General Fyord? My father knew about Sytal's crimes?"

Feya's heart stopped. General Fyord was Strauth's father? He'd told her Morzaun was responsible for his father's death, but she'd assumed the man had been a soldier, not the general. "General Fyord was your father?"

"Yes, and we were told that Morzaun murdered him when he tried to defend the princess. Feya, what you claim—if my father told them about Senniva's death, if he knew it was by Sytal's hands—then why did he lose his life? It doesn't make sense."

Doubt had spread to his eyes. She could see it in his piercing gaze. "Your father found letters that marked Sytal as a traitor. Years ago, mercenaries attacked Izarden. My uncle spent much of his career in Izarden's army searching for the person responsible. Sytal was the man who hired them, Strauth, and your father found out about it. He planned to take the evidence to the people, knowing they would overthrow him. But when my father and uncle arrived at the palace and he told them..."

Tears spilled over her cheeks. All of her own fears fought to the surface, and she struggled to keep them from paralyzing her. "When he told them, my uncle lost control of his powers. Papa managed to shield himself, but your father...he was caught in the blast. My uncle never meant to kill General Fyord. He was their friend—their ally."

Strauth pulled his hand from beneath hers and stood. He shook his head, but it wasn't anger that blanketed his expression. He appeared confused...and hurt. Did he even believe her?

Strauth retreated to the door, and Feya darted after him. She grabbed his arm, and he stopped to look at her. "Strauth, I'm so sorry. This doesn't excuse what my uncle did, but you deserved to know the truth."

His gaze fell to where her hand touched his arm. He pulled it gently from beneath her fingers, and without a word, left her chamber. Had she made a mistake? Feya stumbled back and collapsed onto the bench. Pulling her knees up, she leaned against the window.

No. She couldn't regret telling him the truth, even if it caused them both pain. Even if it meant she would lose him. The lieutenant likely wouldn't believe her version of the event, anyway. Why should he? He'd said so himself; he'd never believe the word of a witch. Why that fact mattered to her so much, she may never understand, but it had carved a hole in her heart.

She *needed* Strauth to believe her.

CHAPTER FIFTEEN
Decisions, Letters, and Biscuits

Strauth leaned against the wall, ruffling his hair. His other hand tapped against his leg. He'd already paced the length of his room more times than he could count, and he still hadn't expelled the excess energy making his heart pound.

Feya's version of the incident leading up to his father's death had played repeatedly in his head since yesterday. How could so many parts of the same story be different, almost as if they were two separate events?

There was really only one explanation—one version had been falsified with twisted truths, and Strauth suspected he knew which of the two was guilty. Too much of Feya's version made sense for him to ignore. He'd always wondered how things had gone wrong so quickly involving those who wielded magic and wondered why they had turned on their own people after years of helping them. Listening to Feya recount the details regarding his father's death wasn't easy, but he now understood why she feared her power.

Feya didn't want to end up like Morzaun. She feared losing control and hurting someone as he had. Morzaun had committed terrible crimes, murdered hundreds of innocent men, but he hadn't gone to the palace intending to kill Strauth's father or the princess. Did that make a difference? Did the circumstances matter when the outcome was the same?

Yes. They did.

At least to Strauth.

He believed Feya had spoken the truth. Everything inside him said she wouldn't lie about this. King Sytal had fooled the people of Izarden, blaming magic for something he had done. The notion didn't sit well with Strauth, and he couldn't help but wonder if Delran was aware of his father's misdeeds.

And what of Ivrin? What would he think when he learned the truth? He and his brother weren't close, but surely the man would not take such lies well? Their father had died uncovering the dark schemes of the former king. If Sytal were responsible for the attack of the mercenaries all those years ago, then that meant he had betrayed his own people.

"I'll write Ivrin a letter," Strauth muttered. "He needs to know the truth."

Strauth sat down at his desk and pulled out a quill and parchment. He kept his letter short, promising more details the next time they met. He also asked that their plan be put on hold. Ivrin hadn't taken well to his last suggestion, but then again, Strauth had just undermined it by saving Feya's life—or attempting to—and that interference had cost his brother a great deal of coin. It had cost Strauth too. Ivrin had ordered him to pay the assassin for a second attempt. Everything his father had left him had gone to paying someone to murder a woman he believed innocent of any wrongdoing. The thought made him nauseous. What would his father have thought? General Fyord had been an honorable man, that much Strauth knew, even if he'd never had much opportunity to get to know him.

His father had been highly respected by the people, and Strauth wanted to follow in his footsteps. Strauth mussed his hair again. "Which is why the assassin also got a letter."

He signed his name to the bottom of his message for Ivrin and rolled the piece. Without those pesky birds, he'd have to find a messenger and hope them capable of locating his brother. They were constantly on the move searching for Morzaun, and now, Feya's brother, Zeeran.

Getting the bounty to the assassin had been simple enough with Ivrin's instructions, but Strauth had sent her directives of his own. He'd told her to keep the money and leave Feya alone, cutting all ties and dealings with the assailant. Ivrin would be furious when he found out, assuming he ever did. Perhaps Strauth would get lucky and the assassin would disappear without a trace.

Strauth pulled out another piece of parchment from the desk drawer. He had one more letter to write. His pacing had accomplished one thing—clarity about his growing feelings for the woman in the room next door. How he'd gone from determined hatred to—well, he wasn't ready to admit to anything just yet. Not to himself, and certainly not to Feya. If he wanted to be an honorable man he needed to end one relationship before starting another.

The problem was—Strauth was engaged.

And had been for several years. The arrangement was one his brother had suggested when he'd shown promise climbing the ranks. His betrothed, Edelin, was the daughter of a captain and nobility ran in her blood on her maternal side. At the time, Strauth had seen no reason not to accept an agreement from her father, who had assumed Strauth would make a name for himself, a required stipulation before vows were to be made.

Strauth's appointment to lieutenant had met that condition, and soon preparations for their wedding would begin. Marriage to a woman he hardly knew hadn't bothered him before, but now doubt filled his mind. Strauth had spent a little time with Edelin, and she had seemed a reasonable choice, but was *reasonable* what he wanted? He didn't know anymore.

But he and Edelin needed to have a discussion, and since Ivrin had instructed him not to leave the palace during his last visit, Strauth intended to write her a letter requesting that she come to him. He would sort out his feelings for Feya before then, and if he needed to, would end his engagement. However, he suspected he already knew which direction his heart and mind leaned.

"Ivrin won't be happy if I call it off. He'll be furious." He didn't dare imagine how his brother would react if he found out Strauth cared for Feya. The man might completely lose it, but Strauth couldn't deny the connection he felt with her, one even he didn't fully understand.

Feya incited feelings he'd never experienced before, and every moment spent in her company only made him wish to know her better. Strauth had never felt that with Edelin. She was just...there. An option presented to him that held no flaw. Her company wasn't necessarily displeasing, and she was beautiful in her own right, but...

He dipped his quill and scratched out a curt note. He'd send the message and would meet with her in a few days. That would give him time to make a rational decision. Of course, until then, Strauth needed to spend time with Feya and sort out his emotions.

A smile pulled at his lips, and he shook his head to rid himself of the expression. Confound it. He needn't be so giddy about it.

He sealed his letters and grabbed the book from his table. Strauth tucked it under his arm. He intended to give it to Feya. He knew what spending hours alone felt like and thought it might help her pass the time. Books had seen him through his childhood, and his love of the written word had followed him into adulthood. Perhaps Feya would enjoy it as well.

Strauth paid a messenger to deliver his notes, grabbed two trays from the kitchen, and made his way to Feya's room. The door banged against the wall, and Feya turned around, one hand pulling the comb he'd given her through her long blonde hair. She sat it down on the bed and played with the folds of her dress.

Why did she appear so sad to see him?

After placing their breakfast on the desk, he approached her. She avoided looking at him, and his stomach twisted. "Feya, is something the matter?"

She shook her head, her gaze firmly stuck to the floor. Strauth curled his fingers under her chin and lifted until her striking blue eyes landed on his. He found it hard to take a breath, and that overwhelming desire to kiss her invaded his thoughts. Terrified he might follow through with his mind's demands, he dropped his hand and took a step back.

He cleared his throat. "Please tell me what's bothering you."

Her eyes glazed, but she drew a deep breath, as if determined to keep her emotions in check. "I never meant to upset you. I'm sorry for making you angry with me."

Angry with her? What in Virgamor was she talking about?

"I don't understand. Why do you think I'm angry with you?"

She turned her attention to the door, shifting restlessly on her feet. "You left so abruptly. And then I didn't see you at dinner. I just assumed—"

"No." Strauth stepped forward and grabbed her hands, making her gasp. What a complete muttonhead he'd been. Having been so lost in his thoughts, he hadn't even brought her dinner last night. "I'm sorry for making you think that. I'm not angry with you. The things you told me yesterday were a lot to take in, and I just needed time to process it all. I can't believe I forgot to bring you dinner. You must be starving."

Her lips lifted a little, and his insides took to performing. "Well, you did leave me *your* breakfast. I didn't go hungry."

"You ease my burden of guilt after I left you in such a state? I don't know that I deserve such kindness."

Feya's eyes searched his. "I was afraid you didn't believe me."

Strauth brushed a strand of hair from her face, and she shuddered. "I believe you, Feya. I believed every word the moment you told me."

The relief that spread over her warmed him for reasons he couldn't explain. Her face pinched, as if she were considering something with deep thought, and then Feya dove against him. His hands wrapped around her, and instead of smoldering warmth, his body ignited with flames. Would he ever grow accustomed to the way he reacted to her embrace? Strauth hoped he wouldn't. He quite enjoyed the feeling.

"I'm so glad," she whispered.

His fingers slid up her back to hold her head against his chest, but the movement caused the book to slip from beneath his arm. It landed on the floor with a thud, and Feya pulled away from him.

"What's this?" she asked, bending over to retrieve it and extinguishing his inner flame. Strauth had to force the scowl from his face before she stood upright again. "Have you been raiding the library?"

"No. It's from my personal collection. I brought a few along with me when I first received my assignment. I thought, perhaps, you might enjoy a turn with it. Reading has always helped me pass the time."

Her gaze dropped to the book, and a deep line filled her forehead. "I appreciate the gesture, but I think you ought to keep it." She handed it to him.

"You don't enjoy reading?"

She bit her lip, and Strauth swallowed, chiding himself for focusing on them. "I enjoy stories, but reading..." Her cheeks colored. "It's difficult for me. The letters never seem to want to sit still, and trying to keep up with them proves more frustrating than enjoyable. I hope you won't think too terribly of me for not accepting your gift this time."

"Of course not. And I already have a solution." Her eyes narrowed, but a smile appeared. Virgamor, he liked her smile. "If you like stories, then clearly I just need to read it to you."

Feya looked away, more red tinting her cheeks. "I don't expect you to waste your time doing that, Lieutenant."

"It's my time. I'll use it however I want, and I wish to spend it with you."

"Even if I'm a witch?" Her expression filled with uncertainty. Strauth regretted, to the deepest corner of his being, for calling her that with so much disdain.

"I'm sorry for judging you solely based on your abilities, Feya. It was wrong of me to do so. I don't care that you're a witch—that you have magic—anymore. I enjoy your company."

Strauth took her hand and pulled her towards the bench beneath the window. They sat down, and he opened the book. Feya giggled, and using both hands, covered the pages to block his view. "I think we may want to eat our breakfast first. It will grow cold."

Strauth heaved a dramatic sigh and snapped the book closed. "I suppose if you insist on being logical."

The amusement that danced in her eyes brought a smile to his face. Feya stood, but before he could join her, she leaned forward and placed a kiss on his cheek. His body went rigid at the self-control required to keep himself from lunging after her to return the gesture. Feya smiled, her face displaying a sheepishness that suggested she'd surprised herself with that warm gift on his skin. She moved away from him to the desk, oblivious to the war raging inside him.

If he wasn't careful, he might just kiss her back, and there'd be nothing *sheepish* about it when he did.

Strauth scooted his chair around the desk and sat down next to her rather than across. She watched him intently, and he didn't miss how his proximity brought the gentle lift of her lips. He nudged her with his elbow and then offered her his biscuit.

Feya liked biscuits. She always devoured them first.

She lifted her brows, and he chuckled. "A peace offering, to beg your forgiveness for not bringing you dinner last night."

For a moment, she wrinkled her nose, and when she finally accepted the flaky bread, she tore it in half and returned a portion to him. "You are forgiven, but I'm not so greedy as to steal all of your biscuit. It's the best part of breakfast, you know."

"I must disagree. The best part isn't the food at all."

He winked, and her cheeks turned a deep red the likes of which he'd never seen. Perhaps flustering her was the best part.

He had decided to end his engagement to Edelin, but even so,

Strauth wouldn't remain a bachelor for long. He may have given away something much more precious than biscuits to the woman meant to be his enemy.

CHAPTER SIXTEEN

Conversation Etiquette

Feya pulled the comb through her hair a little faster than she should have and the piece snagged on a tangle, making her wince. She'd slept in later than usual, and Strauth would be there any moment with her breakfast.

Not that she needed to look perfect for him. She didn't care what he thought about her appearance.

Repeating the thought didn't stop her from smoothing out her messy strands. How many times had she rolled out of bed on Verascene and ran about the village with no thought of how she looked?

Frequently. There'd been no one there she'd cared to impress, but now... she lowered her comb and shook her head. No matter how much she denied it, she *did* care what Strauth thought. An awful lot, in fact.

He'd spent the last several days reading to her, and they'd gone through three books already. The poor man was likely to lose his voice if they kept this up, and she'd considered asking him to renounce the endeavor, but every time he smiled she'd lost the resolve. He did that more often now, and Feya found herself teasing him in hopes of keeping it there.

The door banged against the wall, and she giggled. Why did he always do that?

He closed the door with his foot while balancing a tray in each hand. "Good morning," he said, placing them on the desk. The smell of fresh biscuits drew her closer—at least that's what she blamed her movement on. The man standing next to the table might have had something to do with it, but she wasn't about to confess that.

"Good morning," said Feya, taking her usual chair. "Thank you for breakfast."

Strauth chuckled and shook his head. "As I've told you the last few days, there is no need to thank me. I'm merely the deliverer. I had no part in making it."

There was a subtle grate to his voice that she couldn't ignore. Reading aloud *had* taken a toll on it. "Well, as the only person who ever sees me, I still must thank you. My guard could simply let me starve, and no one would be any wiser. Nor would they miss me, I'd wager."

He stopped eating and blinked at her. "I would certainly miss you."

Her heart lurched into her throat, and she dropped her gaze. He couldn't mean that. Though they were friends now, she remained nothing short of a nuisance—an obligation—and the moment his assignment was complete, she'd likely never see him again.

"You mean you would miss my teasing, as it would leave you rather bored. I know you can't possibly enjoy this assignment, Strauth. A lieutenant must have far more important things he wishes to accomplish than guarding me."

"There are many things I wish to accomplish, but as of late, those things have changed to involve the woman sitting across from me."

Feya lifted her gaze, expecting to find his expression filled with mirth, but she found none. What did he mean by that? His serious display disappeared with the lift of his lips on one side. "For instance, I've wanted to re-read my entire book collection for some time, and you've given me an excuse to do so."

She forced a chuckle, but something inside her fell at his needling. "Speaking of which, I think you ought to take a break from reading today. Your voice grows tired. I can hear it."

His face crumpled. Was he disappointed? "I insist on finishing the one we started. There are but a few chapters remaining. My voice can handle that much."

Elation swelled in her chest. He insisted on finishing. Her happy bubble burst as quickly as it had come. Would that mean the last of their reading together? Feya enjoyed her time with him, and she wasn't ready to return to hours of loneliness that consisted of him only visiting long enough to have a meal. "Very well then. I'm looking forward to how the story will turn out."

"I must admit, watching your reactions when I already know the ending is quite entertaining, especially when you gasp in surprise."

Feya wrinkled her nose and sent him a fake scowl, making him laugh.

"I believe you'll like the way this particular story ends," he said. "It's very romantic."

"What makes you assume I like romance?"

"Don't all women?"

"No." Feya shifted in her chair. True, not all members of the female race liked stories of charming princes or handsome woodsmen, but she did. She couldn't help it. Admitting that to Strauth, however, would only result in her embarrassment.

The knowing look in his eyes made her squirm. Strauth leaned forward slowly, invading her side of the table, and lifted one of his brows. Her heart stuttered. "Do *you* enjoy love stories, Miss Feya?"

How could she not when someone with a silky voice like Strauth's read them to her? Feya lifted her chin. "Only on occasion, Lieutenant."

A lopsided smirk pulled at his lips. Virgamor, her heart might pound completely out of her chest. Did the man know what his smile did to her? One thing was certain—she had no intention of making him aware of the matter.

Strauth leaned back in his chair, an all too satisfied look on his face. Feya focused on finishing her breakfast, but that wasn't easy with him staring at her the way he was: with those steel-blue eyes and folded arms that showed off the sculpted muscles lurking beneath the fabric of his black shirt.

She chided herself for even taking notice of such a thing.

Once her tray was empty, Strauth stood and moved to her side of the table. "Shall we?" he asked, offering her his free hand. The other held the book they were currently reading—the one that apparently had a romantic ending. Not that the whole thing hadn't been that way, but if he had made a point of mentioning it, what did that say about the finale? Had the rest not been romantic to Strauth? Maybe his idea of romance was different?

She pushed the pestering questions out of her mind. Over thinking such things would do her no good.

Feya took his hand, and they sat down on the bench beneath the window. He opened the book and began reading where he'd left off the day before. Strauth's deep voice flowed over her, soothing her soul, and soon he'd reached the end. "And perhaps that is why he loved her. She did not bend to the will of kings nor tyrants, but stood firm in her ideals that the world could build peace on compassion and understanding. Seasons had brought change to the land, but his heart had never wavered. His soul had never ceased yearning to be near her."

Feya sighed, and Strauth paused to flash her a smirk and a raised brow. She scowled. "Oh, stop your teasing and keep reading."

Strauth chuckled and continued on. Without thinking, her head fell to rest against his shoulder, and her heart stopped, along with Strauth's voice. She would just have to blame the story for her muddled emotions. She'd look him in the eyes and tell him it was his own fault for reading it to her with his sultry voice.

Before she could lift her head to say as much, Strauth rested his cheek against her. He breathed in deeply and kept reading. "His energy had been spent on the perils of battle, but he could not rest until the words that haunted his mind were spoken. Drawing her near, he pressed his lips to hers and then whispered in her ear the song of his heart. May we never part, my dear. I love you."

Silence spread through the room. Part of her wanted to pull away and end the awkwardness that rested between them, but part of her also wanted the moment to last forever. Images of the characters in a deep display of affection filled her mind, and without warning, the man's face shifted to Strauth's.

Virgamor!

Feya bolted upright and began wadding the folds of her dress in her hands. Strauth closed the book and shifted to face her. "I'm sorry. Have I made you uncomfortable?"

"No," she answered a little too quickly. "No, you haven't. I was just imagining what that must feel like—to be so fully in love with someone. To kiss them."

Her cheeks burned. Why in Virgamor did she just confess that to Strauth?

He studied her, which did nothing to cool the heat in her face. "You've never been kissed before?"

She swallowed, and her eyes searched the room for something to stare at. "No, I-I have not. There aren't many options where I live." Her gaze wandered back to him. "Have you?"

Feya gasped and shot off the bench towards the center of the room. "Forgive me. I'm being very untoward. I should not have asked you that."

"Seems only fair when I just asked you, but I suppose neither of us is keeping to the proper etiquette of conversation." His brows furrowed. "But yes. I have kissed someone."

Her breakfast curdled in her stomach. Of course, the man had kissed someone. As handsome as he was, it shouldn't have surprised her. Her insides twisted at the notion. Perhaps it wasn't surprise she felt but something else.

Strauth leaned forward and rested his elbows on his knees. "But it wasn't like the characters in the story. It lacked"—he paused to rub his hand over his beard, as if debating the right word—"fervor."

Lacked fervor? Well, that made her feel slightly better, even if it shouldn't have.

Feya shifted her weight. "You must think me silly for visualizing the interactions of fictional people. Men don't waste time on such frivolous things as imagining kisses."

"You have my assurance that you are wrong on that account. Although, we're more likely to imagine kisses with real people over fictional ones."

"That might be true of nobles and princesses, but I can't be persuaded that any man has ever entertained such thoughts about me."

Strauth rubbed his hand over his beard a second time with a conflicted look in his eyes. "Again, I must offer my assurance that your statement is inaccurate. I know of at least one who has."

She gaped. Did he just admit to—

Strauth cleared his throat. "So what are we to spend the afternoon doing if not reading?"

Was he really going to just pretend that conversation hadn't happened? Now all she could think about was spending time with his lips. She restrained the urge to fan her face. "I...you intend to stay?"

"Unless you'd like me to leave?"

She shook her head, still trying to sort out the conversation they'd left behind. Strauth patted the padded cushion on the bench, and her body moved without thinking. She plopped down next to him.

"You know I enjoy reading in my spare time," he said, shifting sideways until his knee touched hers, "but what do you typically do? When you're not being held prisoner, that is."

Feya tried to ignore the way her skin tingled, but it was thoroughly distracting. As if her thoughts weren't befuddled enough already. "I enjoy spending time in the meadow near my home. Picking flowers, sunbathing, the feel of the grass, smell of the sea—I miss being outside."

"You live near the sea?"

She pinched her lips. She shouldn't be giving him so much information.

Strauth sighed. "You don't have to tell me where you live, Feya. Your family has been in hiding for years. I don't expect you to trust me with that information."

"But I do trust you."

That devious smile of his returned. "Enough to allow me to read you stories of romance and ask me questions about kissing."

Her face had never felt so hot. "You enjoy flustering me, don't you?"

"Consider it retribution for how often you do the same to me."

Feya folded her arms. "I didn't realize I did, and I've never done so intentionally."

He chuckled, and the sound swept away any irritation she had tried to retain. "I never said you did, but that doesn't mean I don't enjoy getting my revenge."

She scoffed. "Why *do* we fluster each other so terribly?"

The laughter faded from his expression. She hadn't meant it to be a serious question, nor for Strauth to respond, but that look in his eyes made her desperately want him to answer. His fingers curled around her hand, sending a wave of chills through her body.

"I cannot answer that question today, but I beg of you to ask me again tomorrow." Her brows furrowed, and Strauth brought her hand to his lips. He brushed them so gently against her knuckles that she thought she might have imagined it, but then he did so again, this time lingering long enough for his breath to warm her skin.

She forgot how to breathe.

"I think it best I leave you now, Feya, but I'll see you at dinner."

Nodding was the only thing she seemed capable of doing.

He stood, still holding her hand. Strauth gave it one last squeeze before sliding his fingers free, and disappearing into the corridor with their empty trays.

She hadn't been hungry before now, but suddenly dinner couldn't come soon enough.

CHAPTER SEVENTEEN

All's Well That Ends...

Strauth walked the length of the corridor with a pounding heart. Yesterday, he'd told Feya to ask him her question again today, and the idea of answering, of telling her how he felt, made him giddy. This morning, he'd left Feya to have breakfast on her own, excusing himself to attend to urgent business. It certainly was that. If he meant to retain his honor and not offer affection to a girl he wasn't betrothed to, then he needed to rescind his agreement with Edelin.

She'd responded to his letter, stating she would meet him this morning in the courtyard. More specifically, a part of the courtyard Feya wouldn't be able to see from her window. Strauth couldn't go much farther than that under Ivrin's orders, but he didn't need to. There was no sense in dragging out the conversation, and since the two of them had no actual feelings for each other, parting ways should be simple enough.

At least, he hoped so.

Strauth stopped to peek out the window near the front entry. Edelin stood near the vine covered arch that led into the gardens. Her hair was pinned in a tight coiffure on the top of her head with a few blonde strands hanging down to frame her face. Her elegant gown, with its gold trimmed seams and elaborate embroidery, spoke to her family's wealth.

A wealth Strauth would be walking away from in mere moments.

He'd never taken the time to consider a different option than the one offered him. Being connected to a family such as Edelin's was the dream of many men, not to mention she was the epitome of what society considered beautiful. She held herself with the sophistication and pride of any noble woman, and Strauth had thought himself fortunate to have such a woman. Ivrin had even spoken of his approval of the match, one of the few things Strauth had ever done to earn his regard.

Strauth had never seen his impending marriage as anything more than a suitable agreement. After all, his parents' marriage had been nothing more than an arrangement. They had never been in love. Most people of his acquaintance had settled for a marriage of fortune and opportunity. Love was something found only in the pages of his books. Or so he'd thought.

Strauth stepped through the north entry and out onto the stone pavers. Edelin turned to face him at the sound of his boots tapping against the walkway.

"Lieutenant Strauth," she said, dipping into a curtsy. "How are you?"

"I'm well. And how are you, Miss Edelin? You look as lovely as ever."

She lifted her chin, and her eyes raked over him. His stomach twisted. Why was he constantly being scrutinized? "One does not go about in public without looking their best, Lieutenant, as you would do well to remember, but I appreciate you taking the time to notice. I am very well indeed. Admittedly, a bit surprised to hear from you, and even more so at your request that *I* should come to you."

"I hope you will forgive me for that. Under my current assignment, I am not permitted to leave the palace grounds. There is something I wished to discuss with you that went beyond what words in a letter could convey. Something important."

"Oh? And what might that be? Do you have input regarding our wedding preparations?"

Strauth cleared his throat. The preparations had already begun? Of course they had. Edelin's mother had likely been preparing since the moment he had accepted her father's proposal of marriage to his daughter.

"I suppose you could say that. I wish for the preparations to cease entirely."

Her eyes narrowed, and his lungs lost the ability to expand. "I beg your pardon?"

He took a step towards her and reached for her hands, but Edelin tucked them against her stomach. She'd never been comfortable with his touch, or perhaps hadn't been inclined to allow it. Would she have been that way even after their marriage? "Miss Edelin, I hope you will forgive me for being so blunt, but I do not wish to make this any more dramatic than it needs to be. I can no longer, in good conscience, marry you."

"Why? If you are to desert me after three years of—"

"Of us hardly speaking to one another? Surely my withdrawal does not sadden you? Your father made this arrangement—"

"And you agreed to it!" She stepped closer to him, leaving very little space to separate their bodies. "Our wedding has been the talk of Izarden for months. Do you have any idea what this will do to my reputation...to yours? Does that not bother you? Perhaps you have not considered how this will affect you."

At one time, his answer would have been a resounding *yes*, but his reputation no longer warranted concern. Should he proceed with courting Feya, whatever remained of it would likely disintegrate. Magic wielders weren't held in high esteem among even the lowest classes in Izarden, not just the nobility.

"I'm not worried about my reputation, and I'm quite certain yours will recover without difficulty."

"I don't understand why you would throw away this opportunity. Do you have any idea how many suitors I've turned away since our betrothal? And you wish to just end it? I waited for you to fulfill my father's stipulations, and not so you could just change your mind."

"It sounds as though you will have no trouble replacing me then."

She scoffed and backed away from him. "I would have replaced you months ago had my father not persuaded me otherwise, had he not told me you would soon rank just beneath him. Your title is the only thing of any use to me."

Strauth strangled a laugh. How in Virgamor had he not seen the err in accepting this arrangement before now? Feya may never realize it, but she'd saved him from a life of misery.

"Well, if that is the case, you should be thanking me for not keeping you under obligation. Find someone you deem more suitable, Edelin. I think it best for both of us to do so."

"Do you honestly think you will find a better—" A grin too wicked for such an innocent face spread over her lips. "You already found someone, didn't you? That's why you wished to meet with me so hastily. Tell me, Lieutenant. Who is the fortunate young woman who has stolen you away from me?"

His stomach knotted. Strauth didn't care if people knew who he intended to court, but he preferred to discuss the matter with Feya first. After all, she might completely reject his advances, though his heart told him she wouldn't. Regardless, he could handle the gossip and disdain that would come of the rumors Edelin would likely spread, but he didn't want that for Feya. She had enough hatred to deal with already.

"As our relationship has concluded, you've no reason to be concerned with my personal life." He dipped into a bow. "Good day and goodbye, Miss Edelin."

Edelin glared at him. "You will regret this, Lieutenant."

Strauth shook his head and spun around, mumbling under his breath. "I don't think I shall."

He made his way into the palace, frustration still pricking his skin. How could he have been so oblivious? How could he have thought he would be happy with her? The answer was simple. He hadn't thought about his happiness, at least not *real* happiness. Strauth hadn't thought about finding love.

A smile pulled at his lips. Somehow he'd still found it, and in the last place he'd expected. Now that his engagement had ended, he could tell Feya how he felt. He could kiss her, and Strauth suspected it wouldn't be lacking in anything like his kiss with Edelin.

He'd performed the gesture just once, more out of curiosity than anything. When they'd walked through the gardens of her family's estate, Strauth had taken their moment of solitude to steal a kiss. The whole thing had been rather flat, and not just for him. Edelin hadn't pushed him away, but she certainly hadn't returned his efforts either. After, she'd given him a look that suggested she'd put up with him, but there wouldn't be any notions of romantic exchanges beyond what their marriage required of her.

With Feya things were different. He wanted to kiss her— sometimes, quite desperately.

"Lieutenant."

Delran's deep voice pulled him from his thoughts, and he halted to dip into a bow. "My King."

"Where have you been? I sent several guards to request your presence and they could not locate you. Were you not under strict orders to remain at the palace?"

"My apologies, Your Highness. I had some pressing business to take care of. I asked my party to meet me in the courtyard so as to not disobey your instructions."

Delran's eyes narrowed. "And with whom were you meeting that such business could not be done by letter?"

He wasn't about to go into details with the king. Of what interest of his was it, anyway? "I needed to meet with my betrothed." Bile rose in his throat. Thinking of Edelin in that way made him sick, but Delran needn't know that. "She is planning a wedding. As you can imagine, such things would require far too much parchment."

Delran's mouth twitched, and the tightness in Strauth's chest eased. "I suppose that's an accurate statement, Lieutenant. Best those matters are discussed in person."

Sunlight seeped through the purple curtains, covering the window of the corridor and glistened off the gold buttons on the king's coat. Deep lines formed on his forehead. Strauth had a sinking feeling in the pit of his stomach. "You said you had guards looking for me. Is there something urgent I may help you with, My King?"

"The witch. You are to bring her to the west wing at once."

"The west wing?"

"My son has taken ill, and she *will* heal him."

Strauth swallowed. That statement sounded like it had ended with an unspoken *or else*. Feya struggled to use her powers. She'd barely been able to save him after the assassin left a nice gash in his stomach. No one but Ivrin and Feya knew how badly Strauth had been injured that night, and Strauth doubted telling the king she may not be able to save the prince was a good idea.

Delran stormed past him, but paused after a few steps with his back to Strauth. "Bring her to the west wing immediately, Lieutenant. And tell her she'd better cooperate. She will share the outcome with my son. If he dies, so does she."

CHAPTER EIGHTEEN

Healing Unseen Wounds

Eating breakfast might not have been the best idea. Feya wrapped her arms around her midsection, as if doing so might hold the contents of her stomach in place. Her mind hadn't rested since Strauth left soft kisses on her knuckles the day before—the thought of which had her skin burning all over again—and she'd tossed and turned all night, contemplating his request.

Ask him again tomorrow? What in Virgamor had the man meant by such things? What sort of game was he playing with her heart?

Chills slithered across her skin, and her body shook with a hard shudder. Her heart. Yes, somehow her loathsome lieutenant had found his way into it. She still couldn't understand how, or even when. They'd been determined to dislike each other the moment he had first entered her room and brought her breakfast, and yet somehow they had ended up here.

Feya twisted her hair around her finger and stepped closer to the window. Where exactly was *here*? Every time the man stepped into the room now her pulse raced. He muddled her thoughts with his smiles, and when they touched...

Her body shuddered again.

She had come to care for Strauth in a way she'd never cared for anyone before, and based on his confession, he must have feelings for her as well. He'd admitted to thinking about kissing her.

Heat filled her cheeks, and she shook the image of him scooping her into his arms and performing the gesture from her mind. Just because he'd thought about it didn't mean it would ever happen. Strauth was a lieutenant in Izarden's army, a subject and servant to a king who despised magic. How could a relationship with him possibly work?

She scanned the courtyard, frustrated with the emotions raging through her thoughts. There were several servants below, building something with pieces of wood, while another appeared to be sharpening a long piece of metal nearby under the demands of a guard. Feya had never seen much occur outside her window beyond patrolling guards, so the sight left her curious. Just not curious enough to distract her from thoughts about the lieutenant.

Feya plopped down on her bed, but she barely had time to get comfortable on the velvet blankets before the door swung open with its usual resounding bang against the wall. Feya jumped to her feet and bounded to Strauth's side before he could even seal them inside.

Goodness, she needed to get a hold on her emotions.

Her excitement quickly subsided when he turned to face her with pinched brows. "Is something wrong?" she asked.

Strauth rubbed his hand over his face and began pacing the room. His anxious energy filled the space, doing nothing to ease her nerves. She grabbed his arm and pulled him to a stop.

"Strauth, you're scaring me. What has you so bothered?"

He slid out of her grasp and moved to the window. Strauth peered down into the courtyard, just as she had only minutes before.

"Delran sent me to get you." He looked at her and ran his hand through his hair, disheveling the locks into disarray but somehow only making himself appear more dashing. "The prince has fallen ill, and he expects you to heal him."

"What? But I-I can't! You know I can't!"

"Of course I do, but I wasn't about to tell the king that. Not when—"

He turned back to the window, and Feya rushed to his side. She tilted her head until she could meet his gaze. "Not when what?"

Strauth sighed and nodded to the commotion beyond the paned glass. "Not when he intends to kill you should you fail."

Feya's hands jumped to her mouth, but her gasp still chased away any silence that might have come from such a forlorn statement. What exactly were those men building? She had the notion to ask but decided against it. Knowing what instrument of death awaited her wouldn't comfort her in the slightest.

Strauth pulled her hands away from her face. He held them between his own, and the warmth battled against the cold reality that swept over her.

"You can heal him. I know you can."

She slipped her hands away from him. "No! I can't. I don't have access to my powers. I won't be able to save him!" The room spun, and Feya pressed the back of her hand to her forehead. "I have to get out of here or I'm as good as dead."

"Surely you must know you would never escape? The palace is too heavily guarded."

"What if..." Her words trailed off with her thoughts. Did she dare ask? Well, she didn't have anything to lose. "What if you helped me? The guards know you. They would let you pass, would they not?"

He shook his head, and a sharp jolt struck her heart. "If I thought we'd find success doing that I wouldn't still be standing here with you. Under normal circumstances they may have allowed me to leave, but Delran and Ivrin have me under strict orders not to leave the palace. The entire guard knows that. At minimum, they would be suspicious. Even if we made it out of the gate, we wouldn't get far under such watchful eyes. The punishment would be far worse when we were caught."

Feya wasn't sure how to feel about his response. Disappointment that he couldn't help her warred with the elation she felt that he'd admitted he *would* have helped her had he thought it logical.

Strauth captured her hands again and tugged her closer, pressing her fingers into his chest. "Regardless, I know you can heal him. You saved me."

"That was different. A fluke. I—"

"Feya, listen to me. You don't have a choice. Delran doesn't make idle threats. You have to heal the prince or he'll have you killed, and with his hatred, I can't imagine the method will be a merciful one." For a moment, his gaze flicked to the window, where the guards in the courtyard ordered servants to construct their contraption of death. Strauth lifted his hand to brush a strand of hair from her face, his tone pleading. "You must try."

The lump in her throat burned and threatened to cut off her air. She nodded, any words she could have mustered becoming lost to her sobs. She wrapped her arms around Strauth's waist and rested her head against his chest. His heart pounded as hard as her own beneath his black uniform.

He gave her a strong squeeze and then released her. She hated him for letting go. Feya would have preferred to remain in his embrace, but the king had made a request, and it was Strauth's duty to fulfill it, a painful reminder of why nothing could become of their connection. Strauth's loyalty to Izarden would never allow him to choose her.

"Come," he said, taking her by the hand and leading her towards the door. "Everything will be fine." The shakiness in his tone suggested he held his own doubts.

"And if it's not."

He paused and turned to face her. "I don't—I'll think of something."

The answer only added to her uneasiness. They passed several guards, and each one of them glared at her when they proceeded past them. The reminder of their disdain unsettled her further. They walked the corridors in silence, and Feya focused her attention on the details of the elaborately decorated walls, hoping to distract herself. This part of the palace was new to her, and it was clear by the intricate carvings, painting, and tapestries that this wing belonged to those of the highest blood.

Strauth stopped outside a room, whose door featured an elegantly carved bird with outstretched wings in its center, similar to the one guarding the throne in the Great Hall. He gave her hand one final squeeze before sliding his fingers up her arm, leaving chills in their wake. They curled around her tiny arm muscles with gentleness, but she wondered if he would put on an act as he had during her last meeting with the king.

Strauth rapped a few light taps against the door, and moments later, a servant gestured them inside. Several women bustled about the room, and one stood beside the young prince—who lay expressionless with his eyes closed on the bed—patting a damp cloth to the boy's forehead.

King Delran turned away from the window and marched towards them, followed by two guards. Strauth's grip tightened slightly around her arm, and she noticed his body straightened into a rigid stance.

Strauth bent into a bow, and Feya did her best to curtsy without falling victim to her wobbly knees.

"I know you magic wielders are capable of healing," Delran's voice grated over her with a growl. "You will heal my son, or you will face the same fate as him. You try anything more than that, and I'll see to it you regret having ever been born with powers."

"Yes, Your Highness." Little did the man know she already had such regrets. She had for a long time.

Strauth released her, and Delran gestured towards the bed. Feya walked towards the young boy, the soldiers on her heels, and the servant moved out of her way. His complexion held an unnaturally white hue, and sweat beaded above his brow. Feya placed her hands on his chest, and the excessive heat startled her. How long had the child been ill? Her gaze swept over his youthful face, and sympathy swelled within her at his innocence. She had to help him.

Feya closed her eyes, and the words fell from her lips. Her hands warmed, but only briefly.

She tried again, this time with more fervor, but the result remained the same. Panic invaded every inch of her body. She couldn't do it. Her magic had retreated to a place she couldn't access.

A hand clenched her arm and wheeled her backwards. Delran's dark scowl filled her view, and she felt the depth of his anger radiating from his cold eyes. "I told you what would happen if you didn't obey."

"I—"

"You will be executed for this. I will make an example of you."

She swallowed, trying to ignore the bile rising in her throat. "If you kill me, my family will—"

"Do nothing! I can have a message to my general in a matter of hours. They'll never see the assault coming. I'll order my men to kill them while they sleep. Don't make threats to me, witch. I won't cower under your power. I'm not weak."

Her stomach churned, threatening to spill her morning meal all over the room. His hand tightened around her arm, sending a wave of pain across her shoulder and causing her to cry out. Delran motioned for his guards. "Take her to the courtyard and dispose of her. I've a letter to write."

One of the men reached for her, but Strauth stepped between them. "My King, if I may? I've witnessed this healing spell. With an ailment this severe, it may take some time for its effects to become visible to us. Your son will need to regain his strength, even with magic. It only needs time."

Delran glared at her, as if searching for the truth in his lieutenant's words. She dared not speak, knowing with full certainty her voice would quake. The king pulled her closer. "You have until tomorrow morning. If he hasn't shown signs of improvement, I'll have the guillotine prepared for public execution."

With his hard shove, she collided against Strauth. The lieutenant caught her by the waist, but his hands lingered there only long enough to establish her balance before taking hold of her arm again.

"Take her to her chamber," said Delran."

"Yes, My King."

Strauth bowed and quickly tugged Feya out of the room. His strides were so lengthy that she struggled to keep up with him as he marched back to the guest wing, his gentle touch the complete opposite of the stern look in his expression. Once inside her chamber, Strauth closed the door and pulled up her sleeve. His fingers trailed across her skin, inspecting it with tenderness. "Did he hurt you? If he ever lays a hand on you like that again I might pummel him."

His examination made her thoughts hazy, and her lack of response only drew his brows closer together. "Feya, are you hurt?"

"No, I—you lied to him. You lied to the king! You know my spell doesn't require time. I healed you in a matter of seconds."

"What was I supposed to do? Delran would have sentenced you to death right there and then."

"And now I will be sentenced to death tomorrow, having spent my last hours contemplating my demise!"

He inhaled through his nose and winced. "We have time to fix this before then. We can go back and you can try again."

"Are you mad? Delran won't let me anywhere near the prince again, and even if he did, what difference would it make? I *can't* heal him! No, what I need to do is leave—get out of this palace."

Strauth hadn't locked her door in days, so leaving her chamber wouldn't be an issue. But what of the guards? Sure she'd long since memorized the patrol of the men outside her window, but there would be men around every corner and near every door. She couldn't just *walk* through the entry, and climbing out the window hadn't worked out well the last time.

Perhaps her new sheets were better. Even if they weren't, falling to her death was better than whatever Delran had planned for her.

"Feya, I think you know trying to escape will almost guarantee your death." He tried to grab her hand, but she jerked away. Strauth pinched his lips, and guilt pricked at her heart. "You can heal him. You've already proven yourself capable."

Her eyes burned. Why couldn't he understand that saving him wasn't the same as this? It had taken all of her focus and emotion—all of her heart—to make that spell successful. "This isn't the same, Strauth. I healed you because I couldn't lose you. My magic worked because I *need* you."

His face contorted, but not with the same concern he'd shown her before. Her words had pierced him—deeply. She could see it in his glossy steel-blue eyes as they searched her own. Strauth closed the space between them and took her face between his hands. He pressed his forehead to hers, and Feya's body stiffened with some mixture of excitement and fear—not of the man whom she'd once thought of as her guard and captor, but at what her failure would do to him. Her death would only bring him pain, and she couldn't bear the thought of it.

"This time your magic has to work because *I* need *you*," he whispered, his soft tone sending a shiver down her spine. His lips pressed just below her hairline, and his warm breath tickled her skin. "Please don't give up. I have every confidence that you can do this."

"What if I can't? If I fail, or if they catch us returning to the prince's chamber, they'll punish you right along with me."

"If you fail, then I will do everything I can to get you out of the palace." He slid one hand to the back of her head and wove his fingers through her hair. "You are worth any risk. If I must face an army or stormy sea for you, I will do it."

She chuckled past her sob. "Must you always be so grandiose?"

"I'll have you know I lived a quiet life before I met you." She felt his lips lift against her forehead, and she imagined the smirk that now resided there. "A terribly boring one. If acts of grandeur are what it takes to have you in my life, then so be it."

Her breath caught. Strauth stepped away from her and pulled his sword from his sheath. "You need to practice your magic. Then we can go to the prince's chamber tonight when most everyone's asleep."

Practice? Before she could sort out his meaning, Strauth placed the blade against his hand. He grunted when he slid it over his skin, leaving a line of crimson on his palm. Feya gasped and darted forward. "What are you doing!"

He extended his hand to her, and the sight of his blood made her dizzy with memories. "Heal me." Her brows furrowed, and he tilted his head with a crooked smile. "Unless you'd prefer my injuries be a bit more substantial to encourage performance?"

"That isn't funny. I have no desire for you to hurt yourself just to allow me practice."

Strauth sheathed his sword and took her hand. He placed it over his wound, and she could feel the warmth of the liquid on her skin. "Heal me, Feya."

She could do little to deny his request when he spoke to her in that tone—the same one he'd used to read her stories. Feya focused on where their hands touched and allowed the incantation to pass over her lips.

"It's no use!"

She started to lift her hand, but Strauth's fingers curled around it, keeping it in place. "Try again. If not for yourself, then do it for me."

Did she truly mean so much to him? Warmth filled her chest at the only conclusion that made any sense. She took a deep breath and recited the words again. A steady glow of purple light saturated the room, growing brighter until it flickered and vanished. Feya gaped when she slid her hand away from Strauth's, revealing his stitched skin.

"I knew you could do it," he said, his lips curling.

He may have had faith in her, but Feya hadn't expected to find success, and the surprise nearly overwhelmed her composure. She had little time to relish in the achievement, however. Strauth brought his sword to his hand again, and before she could protest, left another deep cut in his palm.

"Strauth!"

"I told you. Practice."

She gave him a deep scowl before resting her hand over his. This time, the spell performed on her first try. Feya wasn't sure who was happier about that: she or the man with the giddy grin. He moved for his sword, but she stopped him.

"No more of that. I mean it."

"It wouldn't hurt for you—"

"Yes, it *does* hurt. Every single time I watch you. So stop." She lifted her chin and scolded him with her eyes.

He chuckled, and the sound eased the tension in her chest. "All right. If you think you are ready, I'll stop."

She didn't feel prepared in the slightest, but she would not allow him to keep slicing his flesh for her. "Are you certain about this, Strauth? This isn't just dangerous for me. It is for you, too. You could lose your position."

He moved closer, his heat flooding over her like a wave. "When will you understand, Miss Feya, that I am willing to take that risk? A life should always be more important than a title, no matter how insignificant the world may view it. What good is an allegiance to a king that does not value those he rules? A kingdom is built on what those within it are willing to sacrifice their lives to protect, just as a relationship is built on what the participants consider worthy of fighting for, despite whatever hardships and struggles may come. Risking my life to keep you safe, to protect you from Delran or whoever else may threaten you, I do because you mean something to me. You are worth every ounce of energy I can put into the cause."

Strauth leaned forward and pressed his lips to her cheek. Her insides caught fire. She desperately wanted to turn her head, to give him a better reason to risk everything for her. She wanted to kiss him.

He pulled away before she could convince herself to attempt such a thing, but the look in his eyes told her he'd wanted to do more than that simple gesture. She shook the thought from her mind. She shouldn't be thinking about that now.

"I'll return for you tonight," he said. "The guards will take no issue with allowing me to pass. My position does have a few perks we can use to our advantage."

She nodded, unable to say anything more. Strauth was too set on doing this, and after that speech, she could hardly think, let alone respond. She never imagined he would be so willing to fight for her, a magic wielder he'd been bent on hating. So much had changed, and Feya realized that she returned his sentiments completely. She would do anything to keep him safe, to show him he meant just as much to her.

He gave her a smile and slipped out the door, leaving her alone with her thoughts. This morning she'd believed the man found her attractive and perhaps entertaining enough to enjoy her company. Their time together this afternoon had quickly demolished that, taking her own feelings to a new depth. They both might drown before the situation was all sorted.

What she knew for certain was that Lieutenant Strauth had captured her heart.

CHAPTER NINETEEN
This Magic Moment

Strauth closed his door with a soft thud. The light of the lantern flickered against the wall, casting his shadow on the doors of the room across from him in a much larger display than his actual body. He could have been a giant bear the way the dark outline reached from floor to ceiling. Somehow, the notion didn't make him feel any more confident.

His heart pounded. There was too much riding on tonight for him to let his nerves get the better of him. Feya needed him to be strong.

Feya needed him.

Those few spoken words had filled a hole in his heart. He'd never felt anyone needed him before, at least not in the way she did. Strauth had spent most of his life alone, even before his mother and father had passed, and he hadn't realized how deep his desire for companionship truly was. He'd known Feya for just under two weeks, but there existed a connection between them he couldn't deny. He longed to protect her, to comfort her, to be with her.

The whole situation had taken Strauth by surprise. He would have never imagined falling in love with Feya—the woman who had been his enemy not so long ago. Of course, that had been by no fault of her own. Aldeth and his family had sought a pardon, while Strauth and his brother had planned to put an end to magic.

He shook his head at the reminder. He'd been terribly wrong about them. Well, wrong about all of them except Morzaun. The accident that killed his father aside, the man had committed egregious crimes against Izarden. Hundreds of families still deserved justice.

Strauth pushed open the door to Feya's room, holding tight to the knob. A glimmer of light glowed from the desk next to the window, and Feya sat on the bench staring out at the starry sky. He closed the door and made his way over to her. Even in the dim light, he could see the lines of deep concern in her petite features.

He touched her shoulder, and she started, nearly knocking the lantern out of his hand.

"Strauth!" she chided in a breathy whisper. "What are you doing sneaking up on me?"

"You complain when I slam the door and you complain when I don't. Is there no pleasing you?"

Her scowl made his lips curl.

"You can't tell me you aren't just as anxious about this as I am."

Perhaps she was right. Teasing her right now probably wasn't the best idea.

Strauth took her hand and pulled her from the bench. "Everything is going to be fine. You just need to trust yourself—trust your abilities."

She nodded, but he could see the doubt in her eyes, and though he wanted to have complete faith in her, fear tore at his insides. If this didn't work, he would have to initiate his back-up plan, and it was even more perilous. The odds of them escaping the palace without being caught were slim, and Delran would not take kindly to betrayal.

"Keep close to me. If anyone stops us, let me talk to them…and try not to look so terrified. You'll give us away."

"I can't help that I'm terrified," she said, dropping her gaze.

Strauth curled his fingers under her chin and lifted until the light from his lantern glistened off her eyes the same way sunlight glistened off the sea. "I promise I won't let anything happen to you. After all, that is my assigned duty."

Her lips twitched. "Is that the only reason?"

Strauth pressed his forehead to hers, and Feya's smile widened. "No. And once you've saved the prince, you may ask me your question again."

"As far as motivation goes, that isn't terrible."

"If there's something that might offer more, I'm all ears?"

Color filled her cheeks, and she turned away from him. "We should go. I'm only growing more anxious about the whole thing."

Hiding his smirk proved difficult. Feya wanted him to kiss her. He could sense it, just like he had when he left her earlier that evening. Were it not for the fact that her life was presently in danger, he would have kissed her already. But they both needed to focus. There'd be time for *that* after she'd saved the prince. "All right. Let's go."

Strauth guided her down the dark corridors with nothing more than his small lantern to light their path. The eerie quiet of the palace did nothing to ease his restiveness, and his heart pounded in his ears. Too much could go wrong, but what else could they do? What *would* he do if Feya couldn't heal the prince? He knew their odds of escape were slim, but if that became his only option, he would do what he could to keep her safe. Whether he would succeed was another thing.

They rounded a corner, and his eyes caught on a bulky shadow, making his heart jump. Slowing his pace, Strauth took in the shape of a beak and folded wings. He inhaled. He needed to stay calm, for Feya's sake.

Two guards stood at the entrance to the west wing, and they stiffened upon noticing their approach. Would they allow him to pass? He'd been certain before, but now his stomach knotted. He was a lieutenant, but a new one, and he hadn't earned the respect of those beneath him like Ivrin had. Or perhaps Strauth just wasn't as intimidating as his brother.

"At ease," said Strauth after they offered him a salute.

"Forgive me, Lieutenant, but no one is to have access to this wing without permission from the king." The man passed Feya a stern look of disdain.

Feya's muscles tensed beneath his fingers, but Strauth retained his air of confidence. "Under normal circumstances, I would agree with you, but as the prince has taken ill, and Miss Feya is his only chance for recovery, I'm certain we can make an exception. She has recalled a spell that may heal our king's son, but if you would prefer that she didn't do so—"

"I'd prefer to not let that *witch* anywhere near our king or prince, Lieutenant. Her kind don't do anything but cause problems." His hand tightened on his sword handle.

Strauth would be a hypocrite for chiding the man's comments. Not so long ago, similar things had slipped from his mouth. "I understand your hesitation, but I would not bring her here if I didn't believe it necessary. Our king would prefer his son alive, wouldn't you agree?"

"Of course, Lieutenant." The guard relaxed, dropping his hand from his weapon, and the tightness in Strauth's chest ebbed. The man looked over Feya with suspicious eyes, but nodded. "If you're certain she can help. Just do me a favor and keep a close watch on her, sir."

"By my honor," said Strauth. "I won't let her out of my sight."

The two men parted, allowing them to pass, and some of the weight bearing down on him lifted. For a moment, he hadn't been certain his rank would be enough, and the success offered him a bit of much needed relief. But they were far from finished, and there was nothing he could do to ensure Feya's magic worked.

When they reached the prince's chamber, he hesitated, and Feya flashed him a confused expression. "They'll be a maid tending to him," he whispered. "We can't just barge in, but I've spoken to her. She knows we're coming."

Feya's eyes rounded. "And she's fine with it?"

He tried to keep doubt from finding its way into his expression. The woman assigned to tend to the boy was as concerned about his well being as the king, perhaps more so. Strauth had used that to his advantage. He had confided in her and begged her to allow Feya another chance. Being that Feya's magic was the only thing that could save the boy, the maid had obliged. At least, he believed the agreement had been genuine.

Strauth lifted his hand to knock softly on the door. "I hope my trust is not misplaced."

His words did little to ease the concern that laden her features. The door opened to reveal a young woman with droopy eyes and messy blonde hair pinned to the top of her head. She blinked several times before she seemed to realize she wasn't dreaming. "Lieutenant, please come in."

"Thank you, Madam." Strauth released Feya's arm and gestured for her to enter first. The maid watched her intently, and once the three of them were inside, Strauth closed the door. Several lanterns illuminated the room with a soft glow, and Strauth added their own to the assortment on the desk near the bed. The prince lay in the same position they'd seen him in earlier, pearls of sweat dotting his youthful face.

"Can she really heal him?" the woman asked.

Feya frowned, remaining silent. Strauth stepped forward, giving an answer where it seemed Feya could not. "Yes. She can heal him. I've seen her heal far worse."

The maid only looked partially convinced, but it would have to do.

"Perhaps you might like to take a moment away from all of this, Madam? We will only need but a few minutes."

The woman's brows furrowed, and she shifted, her eyes darting restlessly between him and Feya. "I'd prefer to stay here."

He'd hoped she would accept his offer. Feya may have felt more comfortable without someone else in the room, but it seemed the maid's lack of trust in magic would not allow it. He couldn't blame her. H had once harbored the same feelings.

"Very well, Madam. Feya, if you wouldn't mind." He gestured towards the prince, and she gave him a look that revealed her panic. Fortunately, the maid didn't take notice.

Feya moved to the bedside, and it creaked when she sat down beside the boy. She brushed a strand of his damp brown hair from his face.

"He's in such an awful state," she whispered. "The poor thing."

Compassion filled her expression, and she sighed with another stroke of his hair. Feya pressed her palms to the boy's chest, and words Strauth couldn't understand flowed from her lips. He waited on bated breath.

Nothing.

She repeated the incantation, but her purple aura remained allusive. Her body trembled, and fearing that she might give up completely, Strauth sat down beside her. He could feel the eyes of their observer on him as he wrapped one arm around Feya's waist and placed the other over her hands. Whatever the maid's thoughts were about his actions, she didn't voice them.

Feya turned her head just enough to look at him, their lips only inches apart.

"Don't give up," he whispered, ignoring his desire to eliminate that space completely. "Try again."

Feya took a shaky breath and turned her attention back to the prince. Strauth stroked her arm, unable to do more than offer her comfort and encouragement. This had to work. It just had to. Losing Feya wasn't an option for consideration. He cared too much for her to let Delran sentence her to death for something beyond her control.

The moment the strange words left her lips, a bright purple light flowed from her hands, casting a soft glow around the room. Not once had he ever thought he would believe magic was anything more than dangerous and evil, but watching Feya's light dancing across his hand warmed him to the core. It was beautiful in every sense of the word, like a beacon of hope in the darkness, guiding the prince's spirit to recovery, just like the woman using it had guided him from the depths of his own despair.

The spell ended, and the light dissipated. The prince remained still, his eyes closed. Feya's shoulders slumped, and Strauth's chest constricted. "Try again. It will work. I know it will if you just—"

"It already did." She turned to him again, a slow smile creeping across her face. "He's healed. I added a small sleeping spell so that he could get the rest he needs. It will wear off in an hour or so."

The maid shot forward and placed the back of her hand on the boy's forehead. "His fever has broken! You truly have healed him."

Strauth rose from the bed, and Feya followed suit, but before they could move, the maid wrapped her in a tight embrace. "Thank you," she muttered.

"You're welcome."

Strauth chuckled at the surprise in her voice. Magic was so feared and despised by the people of Izarden that to have someone thank her for using it must have seemed odd to Feya.

The maid returned to the prince's side and stroked his cheek, relief clearly visible in her soft expression.

"I knew you could do it," said Strauth.

Feya pinched her lips and shook her head. "Only because you helped me. Believed in me."

Strauth took her hand, and before giving his actions a second thought, brought it to his lips. They both froze. Strauth dragged his eyes away from Feya to see if the maid had noticed. She sat on the edge of the bed, gaping.

Confound it. She'd definitely noticed.

He quickly released Feya's hand and took a step away from her. He didn't care what the world would think of his relationship with her, but there was a time and place to make it known, and right now wasn't it. Strauth hadn't even revealed the depth of his feelings to Feya yet.

The woman sprang from the bed, shaking her head. "Don't worry, Lieutenant. Your secret is safe with me. I owe you a great debt for saving the boy." Her eyes bounced between them, this time not with disdain, but accompanied by a knowing smile. Heat crept up the back of his neck, and Feya's cheeks turned red.

Strauth cleared his throat. "I should return Miss Feya to her room."

The maid nodded, but the movement didn't erase her grin. Strauth took Feya's hand, and after retrieving their lantern again, led her into the corridor. He released it momentarily as they passed the guards, but snatched it back once they rounded the corner into the guest wing.

The moment he closed her chamber door behind them, relief flooded over him. He sat the lantern down on a nearby shelf and released a heavy sigh. Delran would likely not appreciate him taking Feya out of her room against his orders, but perhaps he would overlook that when he learned of his son's recovery. Strauth could handle a reprimand in exchange for this. They had succeeded. Feya would not be sentenced to death, and—

Her arms wrapped around his neck, shaking his thoughts away before they could finish. "I did it. I can't believe I did it! Thank you, Strauth. I would have failed without you."

Strauth wrapped her in his arms and lifted her from the floor for a moment, causing a full laugh to escape her petite body, one that made him smile. She pulled back when he planted her feet on the ground again, mirroring his expression.

He swiped her hair behind her ear, weaving his fingers through the strands and curling them around her neck. She leaned into his touch and sighed, a reaction that made his heart swell to the point he thought it might burst through his chest. Strauth skimmed his thumb over her lips, and her breath hitched. "Allow me to thank you on behalf of every citizen of Izarden for saving the future king."

He dipped his face to hers, at first merely brushing his mouth over her lips, restraining himself with the last of his self-control. Gently, he pressed his lips against one corner of her mouth and then the other. For a moment, she closed her eyes, and he traced the contours of her face with his fingers. A soft kiss on her upper lip drew open her piercing blue gaze.

Feya lifted on her toes, bringing herself closer, and her fingers slid around his neck into his hair, leaving a trail of fire in their wake. Apparently, she was done waiting for him, capturing his breath with a kiss of her own. Strauth took her waist and pushed her against her chamber door, his body exploding with the passion he'd been restraining. He kissed her deeply, and she returned each one with just as much energy as he gave. He lost track of how many times his lips met hers. Had it been minutes? Hours? Perhaps the sun would soon peek into the window.

Opting to give her swollen lips respite, he moved along her jaw and neck. "I should go," he whispered, though he wasn't certain he could convince himself of any such thing.

"Yes, you should." Her hands only clung tighter to his coat.

Strauth groaned, using all his strength to pull back and rest his forehead to hers. "I have to go, Feya. I may forget how to be a gentleman if I don't."

Her fingers trailed up his neck and over his jaw. "You are a good man, Strauth. And, perhaps, too charming for your own good."

Her sheepish smile did more to his stomach than she could possibly know. "The act is only to impress you. I'm glad it's working."

She giggled. "I don't believe it an act at all, but I'm glad you find impressing me a worthwhile pursuit."

Worthwhile didn't even begin to cover it after those kisses.

Kisses he wanted more of.

He dived back in, allowing himself three more. Feya clutched his coat, pulling him in. "You're doing nothing to help me stop," he mumbled against her cheek.

"Don't expect me to apologize for it."

Strauth chuckled and uncurled her fingers from his attire. With a deep inhale, he took a few steps back, but the distance did little to curb his desire to pull her into his arms again.

"Delran will want to see you in the morning. I'll try to bring you breakfast before then. You should get some rest."

She shook her head. "I'm not certain I'll get an ounce of it."

"Just try." He drummed his fingers against his thigh. "I'll need you to step away from the door." Her brows pinched, and heat crept into his face. Strauth cleared his throat. "I'm afraid if I come close to you again, I'll ruin all my progress in trying to remain a gentleman."

"I see." She smiled and stepped away. "Goodnight, Strauth."

Yes. It certainly had been that.

CHAPTER TWENTY

... Well?

Feya rolled the fabric of her lavender dress between her fingers. Despite her declaration last night, she had slept remarkably well. She suspected not having a death sentence hanging over her shoulders had something to do with that, not to mention her emotional exhaustion after thoroughly kissing Strauth.

Her face warmed at the memories. She'd wanted him to kiss her for some time, imagined it even, but nothing had compared to the real thing. Not that she had experience to compare it to, but there was one thing Feya had no doubt about—that kiss hadn't lacked in fervor. It had taken all her willpower to let him leave, but Strauth was a man of honor. They'd already crossed many lines of propriety by being in a room alone together, not that it was entirely their fault. The king had assigned Strauth to her. The man just hadn't considered his lieutenant might fall in love with his ward.

In love? Was that what had happened? Strauth hadn't said those words, but everything about his kiss had spoken as much to her heart. She couldn't say with certainty what he felt, but she knew where her feelings had landed. Feya loved him, as unlikely as the situation seemed. They'd come so far in such a short amount of time, and it scared her a little, but she couldn't deny what she knew to be true.

A familiar bang echoed through her room, and Strauth appeared in the door frame holding two trays. Feya stood from her bed and folded her arms. "And here I thought you would stop doing that."

Strauth shrugged. "Old habits die hard."

"And why is it a habit?" she asked, sitting down in the chair opposite his.

"You need to eat. Delran has already requested that I bring you to the Great Hall once you've finished."

She scoffed and poked at the pile of steaming sausage in front of her. "Since when does the king give me any courtesy of time? He held little patience for me yesterday."

"I suppose since he woke up to his son having made a full recovery."

Feya dropped her fork. "He's awake?"

Strauth chuckled, and a wide smile stole over his lips. "You seem so surprised by this. Are you not the one responsible for it?"

"Well, yes, but...my mind couldn't help but worry I'd still failed.

I'm not used to successfully performing magic, you know. My brothers were always much more talented at it than I was, and not performing it for a year has done little to help."

Strauth swallowed his food and glanced at her, a mischievous glint in his eyes. "Magic may not be your talent, as you say, but I can think of something much better that you *do* happen to be quite good at."

Her mouth dropped. "If you are referring to a certain *occurrence* from last night, then I don't see how I could be good at it when it was only my first attempt."

He nodded and made a low humming sound as he rubbed a hand over his beard. "You may be right. More practice is certainly needed."

Feya narrowed her eyes. "And I suppose you intend to once again volunteer yourself for me to practice on?"

"I am duty bound to sacrifice myself for the greater good."

She ripped off a piece of her biscuit and threw it at him. Strauth laughed, making her fake scowl deteriorate.

After breakfast, he led her to the Great Hall. King Delran, who'd been in deep discussion with a gentleman with a long silvery beard when they arrived, dismissed the man and rose from his throne. Strauth clasped his hands behind his back and bowed, and Feya dipped into a curtsy. Though she was less nervous than yesterday to meet with the king, she still had to focus on not losing her balance.

"It seems I owe you some gratitude, Miss Feya. My son has made a full recovery."

"I'm glad to hear that, Your Highness."

"I suppose I must offer you something in return for your services—"

"That is not necess—"

"—and Lieutenant Strauth has made an agreeable suggestion on your behalf." Feya glanced at Strauth and caught the subtle twitch of his lips. "Under present circumstances, I cannot offer you much of a reward, but it is my understanding that you enjoy being out of doors. I have restricted you to your chamber these past two weeks for obvious reasons, but I am willing to give you one afternoon."

"You're allowing me to leave the palace?"

"I'm allowing you outside. You will remain within the palace walls, and Lieutenant Strauth will chaperone you, of course."

Feya thought her heart might burst. Strauth had requested this for her? She wanted to throw her arms around him and thank him properly, but that wasn't the best idea with Delran watching. She would have to thank him later with a bit of *practice*.

"Thank you, Your Highness. I gladly accept your offer."

His brows furrowed. "Do not mistake this for trust. If you make any attempt to escape, I will have you fired upon before you can even reconsider the choice. Do you understand?"

"Yes, Your Highness."

"Very well," said Delran, his expression ever stoic. "You may take your leave."

It took everything she had to contain her excitement as they entered the corridor, Strauth's light touch holding her upper arm as he led her past the guards. She could go outside. One afternoon wasn't much, but the thought of enjoying the warmth of the sun and the smell of flowers thrilled her. That she would spend that time with the man beside her only increased her happiness.

Instead of rounding the corner to the guest wing, Strauth took her in the opposite direction. She passed him a confused glance, and he smirked. "I assumed you'd want to make use of your reward straight away."

"The king said this afternoon? It's barely past breakfast."

"I believe he said that for my benefit under the presumption that I would not wish to spend more than a few hours outside with you. As this isn't a luxury we often have, I intend to make the most of it. The gardens here are lovely, and the perfect place for a bit of frivolity."

Passing through the palace entry, the guards all watched her, contempt clear in their glares. The intensity made her squirm. Strauth leaned closer and dipped his chin to her ear. "Don't worry about them. They know not to lay a hand on you."

His words didn't erase her concerns, but walking next to Strauth, she felt safe. He wouldn't let anyone harm her; he'd proven that much. They ambled through the courtyard along the northern wall, and her pulse eased. Feya sucked in a deep breath. This was so different from sitting on her bench with the window open.

Once out of sight of those guarding the entrance, Strauth's hand slid down her arm, and his fingers interlocked with hers.

"So you suggested this reward for your own benefit, then?" she asked. "An afternoon of frivolity for your entertainment."

Strauth turned to her with one eyebrow cocked in his typical devilish look that made her stomach twist. "As if that's not a benefit you will enjoy as well? You have wanted me to kiss you since our conversation about the subject during our readings. Perhaps even before that. So don't put all the blame on me."

"How do you know how long I've wanted you to kiss me?"

They stopped beneath a vine covered arch, and a crooked smile tugged at his lips. "Just look at me. How could you not want to be kissed?"

The drop of her jaw made him laugh. He was right, of course, but that didn't mean she needed to boost his ego further. "I told you when this all began that you didn't offer much of a view. Or have you forgotten?"

"No, I haven't let that particular memory slip away. My only comfort comes in knowing that it was the only time you've ever lied to me." She wrinkled her nose, and Strauth gave it a flick with his finger. "And so did I when I said you offered little to entice my observation."

Her cheeks burned, which only seemed to satisfy the lieutenant more. He nodded past the arch, and Feya followed his gaze. "What do you think?"

She slipped her hand from his and entered the gardens. Rows of lush, tall hedges stretched before her, and an array of multicolored flowers dotted along the stone path down the middle. Trees with white buds shadowed a walkway on the southern side, while the north offered a wall of rose bushes with bright pink and crimson blooms.

"It's beautiful," she whispered. "Thank you for bringing me here."

She darted to a bed of flowers a few feet away and bent down to smell the deep red petals. The scent tickled her nose, and brought with it a wave of memories, a reminder of Verascene. She sighed and closed her eyes as the meadow filled her mind, along with the rainbow of little dots nestled in the lush blades. She missed home.

"Come with me," Strauth whispered into her ear from behind, sending shivers down her spine. He recaptured her hand, all the tease completely gone from his expression, and pulled her down the path. They maneuvered through tall hedges for several minutes until they came to a giant statue of a bird with outstretched wings. Strauth tugged her from the pavers onto the grass, and they disappeared into the shadows behind the stone predator.

He pushed her waist against the cold, dark surface and weaved his fingers through her hair. Her heart raced, and she inhaled a breath of warm air, the sweet smell of flowers filling her nose and adding to her euphoria.

Strauth tilted his head towards her lips.

"Lieutenant!"

His body went rigid at the high-pitched call, and his eyes widened as he pulled away from her. "Lieutenant, I know you're here somewhere! Don't tease me. I saw you come this way."

The sound of footsteps approached them. Strauth leaned close to her, whispering, "Stay here."

Before she could protest, he slipped out of the shadows and onto the walkway. Feya pressed against the stone bird and peeked around its wing just as a woman appeared in front of him.

"There you are," she said, swiping golden ringlets from her face.

"What are you doing hiding out here? I thought your assignment kept you inside the palace?"

"What do you want, Edelin?"

Edelin leaned forward and looked towards Feya, as if she knew someone were hiding just out of view. Feya ducked farther behind the statue, her trembling fingers gripping the crystalline structure.

"Are we alone?" Edelin asked.

Strauth shifted. "Yes."

A coy smile curled her lips, and she took several steps closer to him. Edelin took his coat in her hands and lifted on her toes. "Then I think you know what I want."

"I assure you I don't. I thought I'd made myself clear during our last conversation."

"Come now, Lieutenant," she said, sliding her fingers along his jaw. Strauth flinched, but the woman continued to trace his face. "Don't you remember what happened last time we walked through the gardens. Perhaps I need to give you a reminder?"

Last time? Did Strauth often spend time alone with women in the gardens?

Edelin kissed his neck. Strauth grabbed her wrists and yanked them away from his clothes. "What are you doing? You need to leave."

She puffed out her bottom lip. "Does one need a reason to visit her betrothed?"

The world spun. Feya held her stomach, afraid this morning's meal might end up on the grass. His betrothed? Strauth was engaged?

"We are not—"

His words were lost, and Feya peeked out from behind the bird to see Edelin's lips on his. Strauth pushed her away as Feya exited the shadows, her fists clenched.

"You're engaged?"

The lieutenant's face paled, and he shook his head. "Feya, we are not engaged. You don't—"

"We are. The wedding is set for one month from today. Who might you be?" The woman's eyes raked over her, and she wrapped her arm around Strauth's. "I thought you said we were alone, dearest? Oh, you must be the *witch*. Strauth has told me all about his new assignment. Terrible waste of his talents to be assigned to you. I do hope his reputation will not suffer for it."

"Edelin." Strauth attempted to pull his arm away, but she pinned him in a death grip. "I've already told you—"

"That you *despise* this assignment. I know. No need to play a gentleman with her kind, dear. I'm sure she knows her place. Don't you, witch?"

What a fool she'd been. Suddenly the warm air and sweet scents of the garden held no joy. She needed to escape. She couldn't stay here. Feya spun around, and lifting her skirts, ran. Strauth's voice calling after her only increased her pace, and soon distance muffled it completely. She darted between the hedges for what seemed like hours until she reached the vine-covered archway.

Tears drenched her face, and she struggled to catch her breath. A pang in her heart made her chest ache, like someone had pierced it.

And someone had.

She'd been deceived. Strauth didn't care for her. Feya had healed him, and she'd healed the prince, but even magic couldn't fix a shattered heart.

CHAPTER TWENTY ONE
The Price Paid

Strauth started forward after Feya when she ignored his calls, but a yank on his arm pulled him to a halt. Edelin stared at him with her chin raised and her eyes narrowed to pinpricks. "You don't need to go after her."

He glanced down to where her fingers clung to his coat. "Take your hands off of me."

"Not until you and I have a discussion. I came here to talk some sense into you and what do I find? You frolicking about with *her*."

Frolicking? Perhaps he was giddy around Feya, but he didn't

particularly like Edelin's description. However, that was irrelevant right now.

"We already had our discussion, and now you've ruined my afternoon insisting on another. How dare you insult her that way? Feya has done nothing to you."

"You should be thanking me, Strauth."

He scoffed and tugged his arm away from her, but Edelin held tight and the movement only brought her closer. "Thanking you? Our engagement is over Edelin. Did I not make myself clear?"

"You were perfectly clear, but I will not be made a fool. I suspected you had a thing for the little *witch* the king assigned you to guard. A witch, Strauth! How can you let yourself be seen with her kind?"

"What concern is it to you?" he said with a growl. "We are *not* engaged anymore, Edelin! It's none of your business who I'm with, nor should you care."

"I will not be the laughingstock of Izarden. I will not be the girl who lost her betrothed to a witch—to a traitor!"

Strauth grabbed her hand and pulled it from his clothes. "You can't lose what you never had. I accepted your father's offer, but I never belonged to you, a fact that I'm growing more grateful for by the minute."

"A pretty face has made you delusional. Did you think you could sweep her away, steal a few kisses and no one would be the wiser? Tell me, Strauth. Is that all this is? You can't possibly want more from her than that."

"I'm not delusional, and Feya isn't pretty—she's beautiful,

compassionate, and witty. She's everything you're not. I don't expect you to understand what I want. Not once have we ever spoken of what the other desires, though you've made yourself clear my title is all you ever cared about."

Edelin's expression pinched, and her dark brown eyes bore into him with a fiery glare. "You really are smitten with her, aren't you? But I think there is a reasonable man hiding under those feelings. Surely you know what any relationship with her would mean for you?" She placed her hands on his shoulders and slid them down his chest. "Fortunately for you, I'm rather forgiving. I will forget this nonsense, Lieutenant. You can still have me."

Strauth leaned closer to her face. "I don't want you, and you most certainly will *never* have me. Goodbye, Edelin. This time, don't come back."

He lifted her hands from his body and spun around.

"Lieutenant!"

Strauth looked at her over his shoulder, and the scowl he found almost made him laugh.

"If you walk away, my father will see to it your position changes. Walk away from me, and you'll be walking away without a title. Your brother may be the general, but I'd wager even he won't approve of your relationship with that evil wench."

Heat that had nothing to do with the warm air spread over his skin as he considered her words. Edelin was likely right, and a few weeks ago, he would have cared, but he no longer clung to the desire for Ivrin's approval. If his brother couldn't accept him for who he was, then why should Strauth spend his life under constant scrutiny trying to earn his favor? All he wanted was to be happy. He'd realized that simple notion as he had spent time with Feya. Earning her smiles and laughter had given him more joy and purpose than anything he'd ever accomplished in the military.

Yes, Strauth wanted a life of happiness, and Feya gave him that in armfuls.

His smile seemed to confuse Edelin, which only made the expression grow. "Your threats don't scare me. There are more important things in life than titles."

"I won't just stop with you. I'll make sure she pays for this as well. Plenty of people in this city want her dead."

Strauth stormed back to her, and Edelin's eyes widened at his approach. "Don't you dare threaten her. If any harm befalls Feya as a result of your jealousy, you will regret it. That's a promise. We're done, Edelin. Find someone else to torment."

She opened her mouth to rebuff, but Strauth never gave her the chance. He marched down the stone pathway with enough haste that he quickly moved into a full sprint. He needed to find Feya—needed to explain the situation to her. Keeping his betrothal with Edelin from her had been a mistake, but not an intentional one. Their relationship was so new and had progressed so quickly that time had stolen his chance to sort out his thoughts properly. Strauth had never courted a lady before, and his lack of experience showed. The agreement with Edelin's father had allowed him to skip that stage altogether.

He rounded the corner of the marble wall and approached the palace entry. If he had to guess, Feya would have returned to her room after Delran's earlier threats. He nodded to the guards, coming to a stop in front of them.

"Have you seen the young woman under my guard?" he asked.

"Yes, sir. She came through a few minutes ago. We stopped her—had thought to take her to the dungeon, but she looked rather distraught, what with her tears and all. Begged us to take her to her room. Figgs, here, escorted her back."

Strauth's stomach twisted. The look on Feya's face after Edelin's declaration had torn his heart to pieces. He'd never wanted to hurt her.

Well, he supposed at one time he had, but this was different. *He* was different.

"Thank you," he muttered. "I'll take care of the issue."

As he made his way to Feya's room, he mused over Edelin's words. She had left him with a threat, and though he didn't care if he lost his position as lieutenant, Strauth refused to give Edelin any sort of victory. He would resign before her father could exact revenge on his daughter's behalf, but first, he needed to make sure Feya was all right.

Strauth paused outside of her door. He'd never been more nervous about entering her chamber. What if she refused to speak to him? What if he couldn't make things right?

Deciding to push past his fears and doubts, Strauth opened the door, conscious about keeping a tight hold on the knob. His ears immediately caught the sound of her quiet sobs—one's muffled by the purple blankets on her bed. Feya lay tucked beneath them, her body appearing as a long lump, completely hidden under the velvet folds.

He sat down on the edge of her bed and rested his hand on her shoulder. "Feya."

"Go away," she whispered between sobs.

He winced. He could hear the pain in her voice—a pain he'd caused. "Will you please allow me to explain? It's not what you think."

"You don't know what I think. And what does it matter, anyway? You're engaged. There's nothing to explain."

"I'm not engaged—at least not anymore."

She pulled the blankets down enough to peek out at him through swollen red eyes. "Is that supposed to make me feel better?"

"I'm hoping the truth will." She started to pull the fabric back over her head, but he grabbed the edge and held it to stop her. "I was engaged to Edelin, but I'm not anymore. Our betrothal was an arrangement—one I agreed to several years ago and contingent upon my advancement in rank. I never thought I could do better, Feya. Edelin is the daughter of a captain and has a large dowry. Her family is connected to the nobility."

He went to wipe away her tears, but she flinched away from him. The avoidance was like a knife to his heart. He had to earn back her trust, but what could he say? Perhaps the entire truth would bring her back to him. "The moment I realized I was falling in love with you, I wrote to Edelin. I called off our engagement."

Feya swallowed. "The moment...you're falling in love with me?"

Strauth smiled and shook his head. "I'm far beyond falling, Feya."

She sat up and searched his expression, a spark of hope returning to her own. "Why did she say you were still engaged if you're not?"

"Spite and jealousy are my best guesses. I made my intentions clear, but I suppose she wants what she can't have."

Feya rolled the blanket between her fingers, staring at her hands with pinched brows. "Why would she be jealous of me? She's gorgeous, and has money, and—"

Strauth lifted her chin. "She has every reason to be jealous of you. Can you not see how completely enamored I am with you? You stole me away, and I suspect she will never forgive you for it." He brought her hand to his lips. "And I am ever so grateful that you did. I should have told you about all of this before you became stuck in the middle. I should have protected you from her."

Her nose wrinkled, and when her head came to a rest against his shoulder, a flurry of feathers danced in his stomach. "Yes, you should have told me. I may have to start calling you my loathsome lieutenant again."

Strauth tilted his head back and laughed. "Is that what you wanted to call me in the Great Hall that first day? Before you changed your mind, I mean?"

"You noticed that?"

"I've always found it very hard to *not* notice you, despite my best efforts."

She wrapped her hand around his arm and sighed. "You're charming all the frustration out of me. It's hardly fair."

"Does that mean I am forgiven?"

"It means you're taking strides in the right direction. I require much more than well-placed words."

He chuckled, and she held him tighter. "Do tell me what would appease you completely?"

"A quiet afternoon—one filled with you reading me stories and holding me." Her cheeks tinted, and she nibbled at her lip for a moment, as if debating whether to add more stipulations. "Perhaps a kiss or two."

Strauth pressed his lips to the top of her head before resting his cheek against her hair. "I'll gladly agree to all of those specifications."

Strauth stood, pulling Feya up with him, and guided her to the bench under the window. He grabbed a book from the desk before sitting down. Feya snuggled against him again as he began to read, and they spent the day enjoying one another's company. Strauth gave up on reading when his mouth grew dry, but that didn't stop them from talking, sometimes about the most trivial things, but he welcomed the conversation all the same. He remained next to her until stars had replaced the bright rays of the sun.

When her eyes struggled to stay open, he wrapped his arm around her waist and swept the other under her legs. She held him tight as he carried her to the bed. Laying her down gently, he bid her goodnight and slipped away to his room with renewed elation.

They'd escaped the mess Edelin's efforts had created, but there was still one more thing Strauth needed to do. He made it to his room and sat down at his desk to write his resignation. Strauth had little experience as anything other than a soldier, but he would do whatever it took to provide for the woman in the room next to him. He couldn't remain a lieutenant, even without the consequences of his terminated engagement. The people of Izarden were not ready to accept those who wielded magic, and Feya and her family would need to return to the place they had spent the last few years hiding. Strauth took no issue in following her to wherever that may be.

Finished, he scribbled his name on the bottom of the parchment and had started to seal it when a pecking noise sounded from the window, interrupting him before he could drop the red wax onto the piece. Strauth dashed to the paned glass and flipped up the latch. A bird with red and black feathers flew inside, making several laps around his room before landing on the desk.

His approach encouraged the creature to drop its parcel, and it took flight before he could even retrieve the small, abandoned parchment.

Strauth,

The assassin has received your payment and will make her final attempt tonight. I have instructed the guards to abandon their posts. Stay out of the way.

Ivrin

His heart dove into his stomach. This couldn't be! He'd directed the assassin to take her payment and leave Feya alone. His message had been simple and clear, so why had the woman not followed his instruction? Regardless, he had no time to concern himself about it now.

Strauth dropped the message and darted for the door. He had to get Feya out of the palace before it was too late.

CHAPTER TWENTY TWO
Broken Trust, Abandoned Hearts

A pair of emerald green eyes appeared in the shadows, catching the moonlight that percolated through the window. With one swift motion, the assassin brandished a jagged dagger from her belt. She lunged, and Feya bolted upright, gasping. Someone held her trembling body, although who, she couldn't be sure with the darkness of night fully conquering her chamber.

"Feya."

She relaxed at the sound of Strauth's voice. A dream. It had only been a dream.

"Feya, you must get up. I'm sorry I startled you, but I need to get you out of here."

He hadn't startled her, but... Wait. Was that panic in his voice? Her pulse quickened. Something was wrong. She couldn't see his expression, but she could feel the tightness in his arms.

"What's going on?" she asked.

Strauth pulled the blankets away from her, and taking her hands, helped her from the bed. What would bring him to her chamber in the dead of night?

"I need you to follow me," he whispered. "I'm taking you out of the palace."

"What? Out of the palace? Strauth, what are you talking about? I can't leave. We would both—"

"You're in danger here, Feya. The assassin will return tonight."

Her eyes had adjusted just enough to make out the seriousness in his features. "How do you know the assassin will return?"

His body stiffened beneath her touch. Strauth pulled her against his chest in a tight embrace. "I promise I will explain everything to you once I've gotten you to safety, but for now, I need you to trust me. Please."

"I trust you."

He pulled away and kissed her forehead. "Stay close to me and keep quiet. The guards won't be at their posts, so we shouldn't have any problems leaving as long as we get out of here before she arrives."

The guards wouldn't be at their posts? What in Virgamor was going on?

She had no time to ask. Strauth tugged her out the door and into the dark corridor. They'd made the trip through this hall enough times that familiarity led the way, and when they passed into the foyer, moonlight glistened through the windows to illuminate Strauth's pinched expression.

Just as he'd said, they passed no guards as they made their way into the courtyard. Though the air remained warm, Feya still shivered, and the hair on her arms stood on end. A sense of foreboding flooded over her. What would the king do when he found out she was gone? Surely he would not find escaping an assassin an agreeable excuse? What was worse, Strauth was putting his position on the line, perhaps even his life.

Strauth tucked them into the shadows behind a stone statue and peeked around the edge of the black crystalline structure for several moments. "We have a clear path into Izarden, but we will need to find a place to hide. Where did you and Zeeran stay while the rest of your family first met with Delran?"

A few days ago, Feya would have hesitated to give him such information, but she trusted the man holding her hand. "A barn just outside the city. The man who owns it is a friend of my father's."

"And you trust him?"

"Yes, I do."

Strauth looked her over for a moment and then pulled his arms from his coat sleeves. "Put this on," he said, wrapping it around her. "The black will help keep you from being seen. Perhaps I should have picked a dress of less vibrant color."

"I doubt you were thinking about running from an assassin when you chose."

His lips lifted slightly. "No. I was only thinking of how beautiful you would look in it."

Feya bit her lip, wondering if her warming cheeks were visible in the moonlight. Strauth peeked around the statue once more and drew a deep breath. "All right. Once we leave the palace walls, lead the way to the barn. Move quickly, but don't run. We don't want to catch any unwanted attention."

She nodded, and they left the safety of the shadows. Not a single guard stood by the gate, and their absence only increased the dread churning her stomach. Had the assassin paid them to abandon their duties? That the guards would accept a bribe in exchange for her life did nothing to calm her insides.

Once they were fully free of the palace confines, Feya took the lead, still grasping Strauth's hand tightly in her own. She led him down a long side street, and within minutes they had left the walls of the city behind. The open space beyond the houses and shops left her feeling vulnerable. A forest of tall pines and shadows bordered the road on the right, and a vast stretch of fields extended as far as she could see on the left. Tall stalks of wheat shifted in the gentle breeze, and the movement kept stealing her attention from the path ahead.

"There," she said, whispering and pointing to the outline of a weathered barn when they rounded a bend in the road. Strauth increased his pace so that he walked ahead of her, and they soon reached the building. The hinges creaked as Strauth opened one door just enough for them to slip inside. The smell of animals stole her breath, and she stumbled in the darkness towards the back of the barn.

Their satchels still rested in the shadows where they'd left them, and Feya began rummaging through Zeeran's.

"What are you doing?" Strauth asked, looking over her shoulder.

She pulled out her brother's firesteel and flint and held them out to him. "I'm not skilled at making fire, but I'm assuming you are."

"And what are we to burn?" His brows bunched as he took the items from her. "This isn't exactly a safe place to build a fire."

Feya pulled several lanterns from the satchel, and understanding dawned on Strauth's face. He searched for a metal pail while Feya cleared one area of the floor free of straw. The last thing they needed was to catch the entire barn on fire. Strauth immediately went to work with the firesteel and flint and within a few minutes had enough flame to light the three small lanterns.

Feya placed them on the cleared spot on the floor. The light wasn't much, but in addition to the moonlight trickling in from the loft, it at least chased away most of the shadows.

She stood, and unable to refrain from asking her questions any longer, turned to Strauth. "How did you know the assassin was coming tonight?"

He averted his gaze, his features wrinkling with what looked like guilt. "Because I...I hired her—no, not hired. I paid her."

Feya's skin tingled with chills. "What?"

Strauth moved in front of her and took her hands. "Feya, before you came to Izarden, I hated magic. I wanted justice—no, I wanted revenge for my father's death. I thought all magic was a threat to our kingdom. Ivrin planned to eradicate it, and he asked me to help."

"Eradicate it?" She pulled her hands away and stepped back. "You were planning to kill us?"

His face twisted, and the reaction pierced her heart. "Yes."

"How could you? I-I trusted you."

"I thought your family was involved in my father's death. I thought everyone who wielded magic was evil." She shook her head and turned away from him, but Strauth darted around her. "But then I met you. Feya, you showed me how wrong I was."

"Why did you save me? If you hired the assassin, then why did she attack you, and why did you bother to protect me? You could have gotten exactly what you wanted weeks ago."

"Your death is not what I want. I love you!"

"Stop lying to me!"

Her whole body trembled. She took another step back. "You hired someone to kill me and my family. You were engaged, but now you're not. I don't know what to believe, Strauth."

He hung his head. "Ivrin hired the assassin. I didn't know until after I tried to stop her...until after you healed me. And even if I had known she came at my brother's request, I still would have protected you. It only took a few days in your company to know that my notions about magic were incorrect.

"When I thwarted the assassin's attempt, Ivrin was furious. He ordered me to pay for her services, which had doubled because of my interference. Out of fear that she would retaliate, I did so, but I sent her a message with the money. I told her to take the payment and leave you alone. I thought..."

He ran his hand through his hair and began pacing the path between the horse stalls. Feya pressed her hand to her stomach, her nausea making the room spin. What was she to believe? Strauth had planned to kill her, and the truth shredded her heart.

Strauth stopped, his eyes pleading. "Ivrin sent me another message stating that the assassin would return tonight. That's why I took you from the palace. I can't..." He stepped towards Feya, and her mind screamed she should run, but her heart kept her legs frozen in place. The dim lantern light reflected off of his glassy blue eyes, and her soul yearned to believe him, to trust him.

"I can't lose you. I resigned from my position as lieutenant. I won't follow orders that would bring you or your family harm."

"That doesn't make this better. You betrayed me, Strauth. How can I trust that you're telling me the truth now? You've been lying to me this entire time."

"I know," he choked. "I know, and I hate myself for it. But I promise, on my father's grave, that when I said I loved you, I meant it. I've never felt for anyone the way I feel for you. I—"

A loud *tsk* echoed from the shadows, and the light from the lanterns illuminated the emerald gaze of the assassin as she stepped into the center of the barn. Feya gasped, and Strauth grabbed her arm. He tucked her behind him, shielding her from the woman's view.

"Sounds as though there's a bit of trouble in paradise," the woman said, the words muffled behind her half mask as she sauntered forward. Strauth pushed Feya backwards, and she nearly tripped, but his hold on her arm kept her upright.

"What are you doing here?" asked Strauth. "In my message—"

"You told me to keep the money and leave your little darling alone."

Her laugh sent shivers down Feya's spine. So Strauth *had* tried to keep her safe. The thought eased some of her fear, but that act hardly made up for his plan of murder.

He took another step backwards, putting more distance between them and the assassin. "If you received your instruction, then why did you come?"

She tugged at the black fabric covering her mouth and tossed it to the ground. "To kill her, of course."

"I am the one paying for your services, and I'm ordering you to stand down. I won't let you harm her."

The woman looked at her nails with nonchalance and shrugged. "You know, you and your brother are a great deal alike— presumptuous and easily deceived. He was livid, by the way, when I told him about your little note. Said all sorts of fun things not meant for a lady's ears. Not that he thinks of me as anything of the sort. In fact, I believe he has underestimated me, and so have you, Lieutenant, for thinking it was by your orders that I came for the girl."

Strauth pulled his sword from his sheath. "Then by who's orders?"

The assassin's lips curled, and she pulled a dagger from her belt— the same jagged piece Feya had seen in her dreams. Only now did its familiar shape pull at her memories. "I recognize that. It's been years, but Ladisias forged a dagger just like it, and he gave it to my...my uncle."

Strauth looked at her over his shoulder. "Your uncle?"

The assassin advanced, and Feya's back pressed against the barn wall. "Yes, yes. Her uncle sent me to take care of her. She has something he needs."

"What do you mean?" Feya asked, her heart pounding.

"It will hardly matter in a few moments."

Strauth released her arm and gripped the hilt of his sword with both hands. The assassin chuckled. "You're no match for me, Lieutenant. I've trained my entire life to be a deadly weapon for hire."

"You won't touch her."

"Unless you put up a better fight than last time, you will be disappointed...and quite dead."

Strauth stormed forward, and the assassin brandished a second dagger from her belt. He swung his sword, but she crossed her small blades and stopped his attack. The woman twisted, keeping Strauth's sword trapped between her weapons, and ducked under his arm, contorting it until it was pinned behind him. Strauth yelped when she kicked his calf, and he crumbled to his knees. His sword clattered against the floor, and she plunged both daggers towards his back.

The lieutenant rolled, narrowly escaping her assault, and fumbled through the straw, searching for his sword. The assassin advanced. Strauth flipped onto his back and swung the blade upwards just in time to block the woman's jagged dagger. He caught her wrist, stopping her second weapon just inches above his chest. He grunted when she bore down on him, using all of her body weight.

"This time I'll make sure your wounds are fatal," she said.

"Last time, they were fatal," he said with a growl.

Confusion blanketed her expression. Strauth heaved her sideways, and she slammed to the floor. She hissed as the lieutenant clambered to his feet. The assassin jumped to her feet, slashing at Strauth, who staggered backwards to avoid her deadly assault. She alternated weapons with each swipe, and Strauth dodged as the blades ripped passed him. He evaded every lunge, but the assassin refused to relent. Soon, she would pin him to the wall.

Feya stared down at her hands. She needed to summon her magic; she needed to save Strauth. Whatever choices he had made in the past, she couldn't hold them against him, not when he was willing to offer his life to protect her.

Feya focused on the magical energy that flowed through her veins, ignoring the clank of metal that filled the barn and the movements of Strauth and the assassin as they danced along the stalls. Even the animals stirred with commotion, their whines adding to the noise and disrupting her focus.

Strauth stumbled backwards with a scream, holding his palm against his cheek. Blood seeped between his fingers, and he leaned against a stack of bales. Feya rushed to his side, and the assassin cackled. "I told you, Lieutenant."

"She's too agile," said Strauth, panting. "Your magic—can you use it?"

"I just tried. I can't."

"Which is what makes you the perfect person to experiment on," the woman said in a bemused tone. "Without your power, you're vulnerable." She flipped the jagged dagger with a quick flick of her wrist so that the hilt pointed towards them.

Strauth's chest heaved. "Feya, you must summon your powers. You have to keep trying."

The small gemstone on the handle of the assassin's dagger illuminated, filling the barn with a bright blue glow. Strauth's body tensed, and his jaw dropped.

"Magic? But how—"

"It's the weapon," said Feya, gripping his shirt sleeve. "The gemstones hold magic."

She had to do something. Hand on hand combat was one thing, but Strauth couldn't possibly hold her off with a magic dagger too. Somehow this woman had learned to harness the gem's power, or perhaps, *someone* had taught her.

Feya held out her hands, repeating the words to an incantation in her mind.

But nothing happened. Her aura refused to manifest itself.

Strauth tucked her behind him again as the assassin stepped closer, blue light glistening off the scarred skin of her face. Feya knew the lieutenant would fight to protect her, but between his exhaustion and Morzaun's dagger, her hope evaporated. This was it. They were both going to die at her hands.

The barn doors crashed against the interior walls, one falling completely off its hinges, and a streak of green light flowed into the space. It collided with the assassin and hurled her against a stall. Papa's figure appeared in the lantern light, and Feya's heart launched into her throat.

Papa fired another spell as the woman got to her feet. She dodged, and the energy left a crack in the wooden frame, sending the horse on the other side into a fit of panic. Three more balls of green energy chased the assassin as she darted to the back of the barn, each collision sending clouds of dust into the air. The woman knocked over one of the lanterns, making it roll across the floor, and climbed the ladder into the loft. Flames consumed the dry pieces of straw, setting the floor ablaze.

Papa whirled his hands, drawing the fire to him and condensing it into an orb. He groaned at the exertion, and the suffocated blaze died in a puff of black smoke. Papa raced forward and ascended the ladder, but he stopped at the top, his brow furrowing.

"Feya!"

She turned to see Mama running towards her. Feya darted out from behind Strauth and fell into her mother's embrace. Relief flooded over her.

"Are you all right?" Mama asked, pulling her away.

Feya nodded and slipped back into her mother's arms. It had all happened so quickly she could hardly believe this was real. Her family had returned. They were safe.

"She's gone," said Ladisias from behind Mama. "Ran off into the forest. We'll never catch her in the darkness."

Papa climbed back down the ladder, but rather than come to check on her, stormed right for Strauth. Papa's fist struck his jaw, and Strauth staggered backwards. A green glow illuminated Papa's hands, and he wrapped them around Strauth's neck, making him gag.

"Papa, don't!" Feya ripped away from Mama and pulled at her father's coat. "Let him go!"

"He hired that woman to kill you!" growled Papa, pushing Strauth into the barn wall. "I read the letters!"

"But he tried to stop her! Papa, please let him go!" She tugged at his arm as the color drained from Strauth's face. Strauth didn't even try to fight back, likely left incapacitated by whatever spell Papa was using. "He protected me," she choked. "Please don't hurt him!"

Papa loosened his hold, his aura dissipating, and Strauth crumbled to the floor with a heavy gasp. Feya sobbed, and her body shook so violently she thought she might collapse.

Ladisias appeared at their side. "We need to go. As soon as Delran realizes what's going on, he'll send his army after us." He grabbed Papa's arm when he started for the lieutenant. "Leave him. We have to go."

"Aldeth, he's right," whispered Mama. "Don't lose yourself over this. Let's go home. I don't want to be responsible for any more death."

Strauth sat against the wall, still trying to catch his breath. Blood dripped from the long cut on his face. Papa's chest heaved, and he glared at the lieutenant. "If you ever come near my family again, I'll kill you."

Papa took Feya's hand and tugged her towards the door, but her body refused to follow. How could she leave Strauth like this? He was injured, and sympathy overtook any frustration she held for him.

"Come, Feya," said Papa, pulling on her hand again.

Feya slid out of his hold, and his brows pinched. "I need a moment."

Papa reached for her when she took a step towards Strauth, but Ladisias stopped him with a firm grip on the shoulder. Feya fell to her knees beside the lieutenant. Tears rolled from his eyes, the first of his she'd ever seen.

"I'm so sorry," he whispered.

Whatever anger she still held, melted away, and her own tears broke free. She had no doubt he meant his words, the truth of them clear in his gaze. "I know."

Feya leaned forward and placed her hand on his cheek. He leaned into her touch, and warmth surged through her, like a fire flowing through her veins. Purple light surrounded her hand, and Strauth lifted his to hold it in place. He closed his eyes, as if savoring the moment—the last they would ever share.

He allowed her hand to fall away without objection, revealing, his stitched skin, his blue eyes wet with regret.

The assassin had been unsuccessful at using her dagger, but it still felt like one had penetrated Feya's heart. She'd never felt so torn. But her father would never accept Strauth, no matter how badly she wanted to bring him with them. No matter how much leaving the man she loved behind would rip her soul, their relationship could never be. She'd always known that, yet everything inside her protested.

"Feya," said Papa, his tone filled with a mixture of sternness and confusion. "We must go."

Papa was right, but her body refused to move. How could she leave him? Whatever Strauth had done, she had forgiven him—not because he had asked her too, but because she knew he had tried to make things right. He had done everything he could to protect her. Strauth loved her.

"Go," Strauth whispered, the words deepening the lines in his forehead. "You have to go."

Her lip quivered. "Goodbye, Strauth."

His face twisted, and Feya had to turn away from him to convince herself to rise. She stormed past Papa to the door. She would never step foot into Izarden again but would be leaving her heart within its borders.

CHAPTER TWENTY THREE
Truths and Traitors

Strauth sat on the barn floor, his body stiff and aching. His heart wasn't in any better shape. He'd lost her. He would never see Feya's smile or hold her against him again. Even if he had the strength and will to follow them, Aldeth had left him with a firm threat, and Strauth had no doubt the man *would* kill him.

And he could hardly blame him. Strauth had hired an assassin to kill his daughter, and he'd also held a blade to her throat, an act meant to convince Aldeth to obey Delran's orders. Now he realized that giving such a grand performance hadn't been the best of ideas, but at the time, he hadn't come to terms with his feelings for Feya.

Strauth rubbed his cheek, the feel of Feya's hand on his skin now only a memory. How would he ever lay those moments to rest? Did he even want to?

That he had yet to lift himself up off the floor and return to the palace spoke volumes to answer that question. Strauth would never forget Feya. She had taken his heart with her, and he had no desire to return to his former life.

Or what remained of it.

Strauth had gone against his brother's plan, and that would likely not bode well. He had ended his engagement to Edelin, accepting her threat against his title. Worst of all, he had disobeyed King Delran's orders and taken Feya from the palace. Her family had left without fulfilling their commitment to finding Morzaun, and his role in allowing them to leave would mark him as a traitor. How had his life fallen into complete shambles so quickly?

Through the loft window, tints of blue were conquering the black sky. The stars had faded, and morning drew nigh. Feya and her family had left hours ago, and whatever his new course would be, he needed to start it soon. The king would punish him for his actions, and with nothing left of his reputation, he may even face the gallows.

Strauth pushed himself from the floor and dusted the straw from his pants. He would have to leave Izarden—leave everything he'd ever known—and it only added to the pain weighing on his heart.

"I suppose it is my own fault," he muttered.

And yet he held no regret. Everything he had done was to protect someone undeserving of the hatred and prejudice the entire kingdom sought to display. Feya had done nothing to warrant the poor treatment Delran, Ivrin, and even he had shown her. She deserved better than that—better than him.

The sound of flapping wings drew his attention back to the loft just as a black bird with streaks of yellow above its eyes flew through the window and settled on the barn floor. It hopped through the straw and came to a stop at his feet before dropping a slender piece of rolled parchment. The moment Strauth bent over to pick it up, the little creature fluttered away.

His heart pounded. Was it a message from Ivrin? How had the animal known where to find him? The questions left him unsettled, but there was only one way to find out. Strauth unrolled the tiny slip of paper, holding his breath. A single word graced the page.

Verascene

He read it several times, thinking perhaps he was hallucinating. Why would Ivrin send him this? The only plausible explanation was that he hadn't. This message had come from someone else.

Strauth knew little about the island that rested in the sea east of Izarden other than that the waters surrounding it were treacherous. Few sailors dared go anywhere near its shores, making it almost impossible to reach.

At least not without magic.

Feya had said she lived by the sea. An island few people could reach would make the perfect place to hide. Had this message come from Feya? Did that mean she had forgiven him? Wanted him to follow her?

The pain he'd seen in her expression when she'd left had torn him to pieces, but if this meant she still cared for him, then he would do something rather brash. Aldeth would likely put an end to him the moment Strauth attempted to see his daughter, but he had to try. He had to know if Feya would allow him to be part of her life.

Besides, Aldeth would have been the only one able to send the note with his ability to connect with nature. Perhaps Feya had convinced him that Strauth had only wanted to protect her.

Strauth tucked the parchment into his pocket and slipped out of the barn. The sun would soon peek above the horizon, and that left him little time to gather what he would need for the journey. Finding something from his home to use as barter would be simple enough, but locating a crew willing to accept it and venture near Verascene was another thing entirely.

He would find a way. He wouldn't stop until he had.

The streets of Izarden were quiet in the early morning hours, but soon, people would flood the streets and King Delran would learn of his post abandonment. The army would be dispatched in search of those who wielded magic, and Strauth would likely be wanted as well. That knowledge alone was enough to encourage haste. Within minutes, he arrived at his home—the one he would say goodbye to forever.

Strauth turned the knob and gave the door a push, but the wooden slab didn't budge. He'd meant to fix the stubborn thing forever ago, but time had not permitted it. He groaned and put more effort into the next attempt, using all of his body weight to part it from the frame. It met the inner wall with a loud *bang*, and he winced. Only silence greeted him, and Strauth had to remind himself that Feya was no longer in Izarden to chide him about the habit.

He began rummaging through his things, not bothering to close the door, and filling a cloth sack with what he deemed most important. A few changes of clothing, several pieces of his mother's jewelry—ones that held enough value for bartering—and what little coin he had left were all tossed inside. He would make do without the rest.

A muffled whinny echoed from outside. Strauth darted to the window. A brown stallion stood next to his home, but there was no rider in sight.

"Going somewhere?"

Strauth spun around to face the door. Ivrin stood in the frame, his dark eyes burning with a dangerous glare. He took several steps inside and glanced around the room.

"What is your intention, brother?" asked Ivrin. "Leave Izarden? Flee from your mistakes?"

"I don't see them as mistakes, but the king surely will. I'd prefer to keep breathing, if that's what you're asking."

Ivrin waved a piece of parchment in front of him. "I found this in your chamber at the palace—a resignation—and beside it, my message informing you about the assassin. And then when we found the witch's room vacant, I assumed you had run off with her.

Admittedly, I didn't think you'd be stupid enough to bring her to your home, but here we are. Where is she, Strauth?"

"With her family, where she ought to be."

His brother ran his hand through his silver-streaked hair and shook his head. "Then it is far worse than I feared. You've allowed them all to escape. You're lucky I'm in a position to help you. Delran will not be pleased when he finds out, but he needn't know the details. Convincing him that the young woman bewitched you will be simple enough, what with it being accurate."

"Feya did *not* bewitch me. I chose to protect her, as per my assignment."

"Your *assignment?*" Ivrin marched forward and pressed his finger into Strauth's chest. "You allowed that wench to get inside your head. I told you to be careful! Do you think the assassin will take kindly to you thwarting her, to your interference? She will hunt us both down."

"I told her to leave Feya alone."

"I'm aware! She showed me the note, Strauth. What were you thinking? You were supposed to help me eliminate the threat of magic against Izarden, and instead, you've done the exact opposite!"

Strauth clenched his fists. "Aldeth and his family are not a threat to our kingdom. They only want peace. They are innocent of any wrongdoing. Ivrin, King Sytal lied about what happened that night. Morzaun never killed the princess—Sytal did. He covered up his own traitorous actions by placing the blame on those who use magic."

"Perhaps so, but he still murdered our father and our king."

"I realize that, but our father's death was an accident. Morzaun lost control—" Strauth's thoughts stopped him from continuing. The information he'd just presented to his brother should have left the man in shock, as it had him when Feya revealed the truth, but Ivrin didn't look the least bit surprised. "Did you know about this? Did you know about Sytal's lies?"

Ivrin scoffed and stepped away from him. "Of course, I knew. Father confided everything to me—the mercenaries, Morzaun's refusal to follow his king's commands. He intended to tell the people, to start a rebellion. I begged him to let it go. I told him his crusade would get him killed! And I was right. Morzaun took his life in some fit of rage, and he nearly killed the king that night as well."

"What?"

"Morzaun attacked King Sytal with magic, but Aldeth healed him and fled before anyone could apprehend him. Sytal called me to the Great Hall and divulged everything soon after. Appointed me as the new general with my promise to keep the details quiet."

"How could you accept that position knowing what happened? Knowing Sytal betrayed his own people? And then you told Mother and me that Father died trying to stop Morzaun from murdering the princess. You lied to us!"

"I did what I had to do. Our family's reputation would have been laid to ruin with the truth. We would have lost everything, so I agreed to keep Sytal's secrets, and he rewarded me handsomely for it. Besides, unlike our father, I am loyal to my king. I won't turn my back on Izarden as he did...as you have."

Strauth's stomach knotted. All this time, he had assumed Ivrin unaware of the truth, when in reality, his brother had played a role in keeping the people of Izarden ignorant. Any respect he'd retained for Ivrin vanished. "Loyalty should be earned, and Sytal did nothing to deserve it. Not from our father, not from you, and certainly not from me. I will not stand beside anyone who falsely accuses the innocent and betrays his own people."

"Then you truly are a traitor, and I will deal with you as such."

Ivrin drew his sword, and Strauth barely had time to pull his own before Ivrin swung his blade. The metal clashed, and the sound echoed through morning air. Strauth spun, swiping his blade over his brother's midsection. The tip nicked Ivrin's armor, but did nothing to deter the man from following him. He hadn't thought to put on his own in his rush to get Feya out of the palace. A mistake he might soon regret.

Strauth staggered backwards, nearly tripping over the rug as Ivrin swatted his gold-studded weapon at his limbs. He evaded another swing, but Ivrin jammed his elbow into Strauth's side. Strauth's sword flew from his grip, clanking against the floor and sliding under the table.

Ivrin's sword slid against Strauth's shoulder, sending pain coursing through the left side of his body. Strauth screamed, and Ivrin followed his retreat to the wall. Ivrin lifted his sword, but Strauth balled his fist and punched. A loud *crack* met his ears as his knuckles collided with his brother's face. Ivrin yelled, covering his nose with his hand. Holding his shoulder wound, Strauth dashed behind the table and picked up his sword.

"You'll pay for that!" said Ivrin.

"Add it to the list of everything else you feel I should pay for."

"Surrender, Strauth. It's the only way you come out of this alive."

No, escaping was the only way he'd come out of this alive. Strauth wasn't ignorant as to what became of those deemed traitors. Delran would sentence him to the guillotine faster than a heartbeat. If he wanted any chance of living, he had to get out of Izarden.

Ivrin took a few steps around the table, and Strauth mirrored his movements. "Don't be a fool," said Ivrin. "You know you're no match for me."

That was a truth Strauth had already accepted, but if he could just get a clear line to the door, he might escape his brother. Ivrin's horse still waited outside, and if Strauth could run to the animal, he would have a good enough lead to stand a chance. He just needed a distraction.

"I'm ashamed that you allowed that *witch* to turn you against your own family," spat Ivrin. "You've brought dishonor to yourself, all because that wench tickles some fancy of yours. You had it all, Strauth: a title, an engagement to a woman connected to nobility, and the king's favor."

Strauth slowly sheathed his sword and gripped the underside of the table as he took a step to match his brother's movements. "None of which I have any desire for now."

"You're a fool, just like Father. Couldn't keep your nose out of where it didn't belong. Couldn't follow simple orders."

He'd reached the center of one side of the table now. This was his only chance. "I'd rather be like our father than like you!"

Strauth lifted the edge with all the strength he had left and shoved until the furniture toppled over. Ivrin fumbled backwards but not quickly enough to get out of the way. He tripped, and the table landed on his legs. Strauth bounded for the door.

Ivrin's screams followed him, but he didn't look back to see if his brother had freed himself. Strauth mounted the stallion and raced through the cobblestone streets of Izarden. As he cleared the city gate, Strauth gave one last look to the place he'd once called home. It had never seemed so foreign and cold to him than it did now, but his heart had taken refuge somewhere else, and it was time he built a new home with the person who had set his soul free.

CHAPTER TWENTY FOUR

Home Sick

The silence in the room did nothing to ease the pressure inside Feya's chest. Two days ago, they had landed on the shores of Verascene, and the tension had only continued to mount since then. She'd barely spoken a word about the events in the barn, at least not in regards to healing Strauth. How could she when they wouldn't understand?

Papa had reiterated his disapproval of the lieutenant frequently on their journey home. It had taken everything she had to not rebuff his statements. Feya didn't have the energy to explain the entire situation to them, and she doubted Papa would listen, anyway. His determination to hate Strauth outmatched any she'd seen in him, and she supposed she couldn't fault him for it after everything that had happened. But Papa didn't know Strauth like she did. He hadn't met the man she'd come to love.

For days, she'd tried to push the memories into the far reaches of her mind. If she could forget her time with the lieutenant, things would be easier, but the memories refused to be drowned by anything other than exhaustion. Only when she had relinquished all of her tears did she finally fall asleep each night. Even then, the lieutenant filled her dreams.

Feya lifted her fork and allowed the utensil to hover in front of her mouth for several moments before putting it back down on her plate. She had eaten little since they left Izarden, yet she possessed no desire to fill her stomach.

A warm hand covered her own, pulling her attention away from the unappealing eggs and biscuits. "Feya, you need to eat something," said Mama.

"I'm not hungry."

Mama sighed and turned to Papa, who sat directly across from her. She gave him a pointed look, and Papa set his fork down. "Aslo has asked for help building his new coop. I'll likely be gone till late this afternoon." His gaze dropped back to his plate, and he cleared his throat. "He's also been asking about you, Feya."

Ladisias, who sat next to Papa, shook his head, his eyes wide. He hadn't teased her once since they'd returned home and seemed to be just as concerned as Mama. It also appeared her brother found her father's idea of helping her move on terribly misplaced.

"Then I suppose you'd better give him my regards," said Feya, attempting to keep her tone even.

"Perhaps you might come with me. It would be good for you to—"

"Forget everything that happened? Except his courtship? Put on a happy face?"

"Feya, we've been through this. I don't know what you expect me to say? The general and the lieutenant were planning to kill you. They hired an assassin, and you act as though you...as though you..."

Papa ran his hands through his hair and growled, but she wouldn't back down today. She was tired of pretending.

"Am I acting as though I miss him?" She lifted her chin and met his gaze. "As though I care for him? I'm sorry if that's not what you want to hear, but it's the truth. Regardless, it hardly matters how I feel. I'm to never see the lieutenant again, and our trip to Izarden has ensured that none of us will ever be free to leave this island without fearing for our lives or being tried for treason."

"And you would do well to remember that had your mother not seen a vision of the assassin and had I not acted upon my suspicions and read one of the general's letters, you would not be sitting here."

"Aldeth," Mama whispered.

Papa massaged the bridge of his nose and sighed. When he looked at her again, his expression softened. "I'm sorry, Feya. This is my fault. I never should have left you at the palace. I never should have left you with *him*. Perhaps if I had made better choices, you would not have been in harm's way and Zeeran would still be with us."

He rose and left their cottage without another word. Feya pinched her eyes closed. She'd never been one to be at odds with her father, and she hated the distance between them. Papa blamed himself for Zeeran leaving, and he blamed himself for allowing her to become the target of an assassination. She blamed him for neither, and watching him carry the burden of both only added to the pain weighing on her.

Mama patted her hand. "I will speak to your father about Aslo. He doesn't mean to push you. I think he's just trying to help in the only way he knows how."

"By encouraging me to court someone I have no interest in?"

The corner of Mama's mouth lifted. "By distracting you with anything within reach. He's having a hard time accepting all of this. Your father is a good man, but he can be a little overprotective. He wasn't always that way, but after everything with your uncle..." Mama clasped her hands and placed them in her lap. "My brother made decisions that led him down a dark path, but your father has always blamed himself for not doing more to help him."

"Mama, I know none of that was his fault. Papa should not feel he has to carry that weight, but he is wrong about the lieutenant. The general contrived the plan, and although Strauth went along with it at first, he later tried to stop it. He tried to protect me."

"And I'm glad he did. We would have surely lost you had he not. Your father knows that; he just...." She bit her lip. "He will come around. Strauth seems like an honorable man."

Ladisias scoffed. "I don't think honor had much to do with it."

Feya's brows pinched. "Strauth is an—"

"I'm not saying that he isn't, just that I don't think honor was the driving force behind his actions. He's clearly smitten with you. Anyone could see it." He took a bite of eggs and shrugged. "Including Papa, which is what has him so bothered, I think. He doesn't know what to do with the fact that the man in love with his daughter is one he doesn't trust."

"I still don't see why it matters," said Feya. "It's not as though he has to worry about it anymore."

"But he *does* worry," replied Mama. "He can see how distraught you are. How much this has affected you."

Mama's concerned eyes stirred her stomach with guilt. She hated making her parents worry, but at the moment, Feya had little control over it. She couldn't just make her feelings go away. As much as she wanted to, she couldn't pick up her life like Strauth had never been a part of it. And she didn't want to.

Ladisias rose and placed his empty dishes in the washbasin. "I'm going down to the shore. I'll be back this afternoon."

"The shore?" asked Mama. "You don't intend to help your father today?"

"No, I intend to do a bit of fishing."

Mama's brows lifted high on her forehead. "Fishing? The last time you tried *that* you came home with three hooks stuck in your back. I think you ought to stick to forging and sword fighting for hobbies."

Feya chuckled, the first laugh she'd managed in days. The corners of Ladisias's eyes crinkled in response. "I don't suspect I'll be doing that sort of fishing today."

He passed Mama a wink, and understanding dawned on her features. Feya hadn't the slightest idea what the two of them were on about, and she hadn't enough energy to work it out. Mentally, she was drained.

"I see," said Mama. "Well, do be careful then. Take a loaf of bread with you, some clothes, and perhaps your sword as well. Just in case."

His sword? What kind of fishing did Mama think Ladisias would be doing?

Her brother rounded the table and kissed Mama on the cheek. To Feya's surprise, he left one on top of her head, too. "I'll see the two of you this afternoon."

Mama sighed once he had left the cottage. "Darling, what can I do to help you feel better?"

Feya lifted her gaze and gave Mama a weak smile. "There isn't anything, I'm afraid. Perhaps time is the only solution."

"When you say you care for the lieutenant, it's more than that, isn't it? You love him?"

Her lip quivered. She'd never admitted it out loud, and now she feared saying the word would only make her heart hurt even more, but she couldn't keep it bottled inside. "Yes, I love him. And I miss him desperately. He's all I think about."

Mama wrapped her arm around Feya's shoulder and pulled her close. "Everything will be fine. You'll see. Tell me what it is about Lieutenant Strauth that you love so much."

She sniffled, and though her heart still ached, something about the confession eased the tightness in her chest. "He makes me laugh...makes me smile even when I don't feel happy. I feel safe when I'm with him, and he reads me stories until his voice is too dry to continue."

Mama stroked her hair, and the gesture filled Feya with much needed warmth. "He sounds like a sweet young man."

"He is. I know he has made mistakes, and I wish Papa knew the real him. Perhaps he wouldn't despise him so much."

"Give him time. Your father only wants what's best for you. He's just struggling to see what that is at the moment."

She had plenty of time—a lifetime of it—but it would make little difference. She would never see Strauth again, and even if Papa came to terms with her affection for the man, the lieutenant would likely move on. It wasn't as though she could go back to Izarden to find him. Too many people wanted her and her family dead.

She also couldn't help but worry about Strauth's well-being. He had taken her out of the palace, and there was a good chance he would be punished for it. Perhaps his brother, in his position as general, would protect him. Strauth was smart enough to make up a story about why he had acted against the king's orders, and the thought of him spouting such lies to preserve his life surprisingly didn't bother her. She didn't care what falsehoods he told, so long as they kept him alive. Strauth could move on, perhaps even marry the young lady from the gardens.

"I was rather surprised, you know," said Mama, brushing her fingers through Feya's hair. "To see you using your magic."

Feya twisted her fingers together. She'd tried to use her power several times since they returned without success. Her magic only reminded her of Strauth and the hole in her heart. She might never use it without thinking of him. Their abilities were directly tied to their emotions, which was why Morzaun had lost control after Sytal had murdered his wife. Memories of the lieutenant only filled her with a bitter sorrow, and because of that, what little control of her magic she'd regained seemed to have fallen back into the dark void inside her.

"Strauth helped me find myself," she whispered. "Without him, I don't know if I can find that part of me again. I think I may have left it in Izarden."

Mama squeezed her. "I'm sorry, sweetheart. I know this must be incredibly difficult for you, but I think you will find that which you have lost, and sooner than you think. Perhaps Lieutenant Strauth isn't through helping you."

What Feya wouldn't have given for that to be true, but she didn't have the strength to rebuff Mama's optimism. "Do you think Zeeran will ever come home?" she asked, hoping to shift the conversation away from Strauth.

"I hope so," replied Mama, choking a little on the words. "If he knew what your uncle did—that he hired the assassin to kill you—I know he would."

Feya had told her parents about her uncle's betrayal, though she still didn't understand why he had sent an assassin to kill her. Mama and Papa had used their power to remove her uncle's ability to wield magic. Perhaps he only sought revenge, but the woman had said Feya possessed something her uncle needed. What she'd meant by that, Feya didn't know.

Feya sat up and drew a shaky breath. "I think I'll go to the meadow today. Perhaps the fresh air will help."

She suspected it wouldn't, but staying cooped up in their cottage certainly wasn't doing her any good.

"Just let me know if there's anything I can do to help."

Feya nodded.

There wasn't anything anyone could do. The only person capable of healing her broken heart lived across the sea. Time and distance may numb her feelings, but she would never forget. She would never fully recover but could learn to live with the pain. At one time, she had been homesick for Verascene, but now that her heart had found a home somewhere else, she worried she may feel that way forever.

CHAPTER TWENTY FIVE

Perils of a Wayward Heart

Strauth's stomach churned as he looked out over the rough seas. In the distance, a mountain of green shot skyward, the peak hidden above the fluffy clouds. Waves crashed against the rocky shoreline with a loud thunder that hurt his ears.

He must be insane.

Who in their right mind would attempt to go ashore in nothing more than a rowboat?

He supposed he would, seeing as how it was his only option. The crew refused to go any closer to Verascene, and now that he'd seen the waters surrounding the island for himself, he could hardly blame them. Any attempt of a ship making a clean beach on the shore would likely leave them stranded, or worse—dead.

For two days, he'd attempted to convince them to try, but now he understood their reluctance. Strauth couldn't ask them to risk their lives, so he'd asked for a rowboat instead.

Strauth had lost count of how many people had laughed in his face at his request to sail to Verascene. He'd almost lost hope of finding anyone at all. Pushing the only men brave enough to offer him passage wasn't a good idea, not to mention they already watched him as though he were mad, and not just because of his travel requests.

Strauth glanced skyward towards the crow's nest. He could just make out the shape of the little bird that had been following him for the past few days. Occasionally, the creature would disappear, only to return and make laps around his head. The crew found the entire ordeal strange, some of them even calling it a bad omen. Strauth, on the other hand, knew someone was keeping tabs on him, and he wasn't certain how he should feel about that.

A man with a grey beard down to his belly approached him. The captain had been reluctant to accept Strauth's request at first, but his crew had fallen on hard times, and Strauth had offered him the only things he had left to give—a strong, able body and his sword. His weapon had been a gift from Ivrin when he'd gained his title, and the craftsmanship was of the finest Izarden could make. The stones embedded in the hilt alone were enough to fetch a fair amount of coin. Strauth had also helped unload their cargo before they headed out to sea, and his efforts seemed to have earned the captain's respect.

"Are you certain about this, boy?" the captain asked.

"No, but I'm going to do it, anyway."

The man rubbed a hand over his mouth, looking Strauth over. "Sure hope your reason for doin' this is worth it. Not that it matters much, o'course. You'll likely be too dead to find out."

Strauth drummed his fingers against his thigh. "I appreciate your confidence. How much closer can you take me?"

He shook his head, making his beard dance across his chest. "This is as far as I dare go. If you'll hop in the boat, my men will lower you down."

Strauth made his way to the wooden skiff dangling over the edge of the ship, the vessel that would likely take him to his death, and climbed inside.

"Last time I'll ask," said the captain. "You sure you want to do this?" Strauth's hands gripped the oars, and he nodded more determinedly than his lack of confidence should have allowed. The captain shrugged. "Best of luck to you, then. Lower him down!"

The boat wobbled and tossed about until it finally met the water. Strauth steadied himself and gripped the oars that threatened to slip over the sides. He began paddling away from the ship, his heart racing more with each stroke that pulled him towards the island. The waves beat against the side of his vessel, sloshing into the boat and filling it with water.

The current pulled him in all directions, and Strauth fought with all the strength he possessed to keep himself on target. The cliff face drew closer, the jagged rocks below like teeth waiting to slash him to bits. Breathing hard, Strauth strained, bringing his arms back and holding the oars. His hands shook, and sweat dripped into his eyes. Waves pounded against the side of his boat and flooded the interior, leaving him drenched in salty seawater.

A jolt flung him forward, and both oars ripped from his hands. Strauth shot forward, but it was too late. They disappeared into the dark depths. The boat jerked and screeched as it passed over the jagged reef hiding just below the surface, and an enormous wave smashed into him, hurtling the vessel against a protruding piece of black rock. The wall of the boat snapped with a loud *crack*, and more water poured inside.

The skiff sank lower, forcing Strauth to battle the waves. The sea tossed Strauth relentlessly between rocks and sharp coral, tearing his clothing and leaving lashes all over his body. He fought to keep above the surface, but his muscles burned with exhaustion and the current pulled him under. Shadows filled his vision. The world above blurred as he plunged farther beneath the waves.

His wayward heart had brought him towards the woman he loved, but it had also brought him to his death.

* * *

His lungs burned as if someone had started a fire on his insides, and the heat spread through his entire body. Before he could make sense of the familiar sensation, he coughed, and water spilled from his mouth, allowing him to breathe in the salty air. Darkness still shadowed his vision, but Strauth could feel the coarse, wet sand beneath him. His fingers dug into it, grounding him to reality.

He hadn't drowned. He hadn't died.

A voice fell over him in a slur of sound, and something smacked repeatedly against his face. Slowly, color swirled into view. A blue sky with streaks of puffy white hovered above him, and the bright rays of the sun made him squint.

"That's right, Lieutenant. Breathe. We can't have you dying after you've come this far."

Who the devil was talking to him?

Strauth pinched his eyes closed for a moment, and when he opened them again, a man with golden blond hair stared down at him. He tried to sit up, but the movement only made everything spin, and he fell back onto the sand with a groan.

"Take it easy. You nearly died, and according to my sister, that would make twice this month."

His sister?

"Ladisias?" he muttered, not completely certain but unable to come up with a better explanation.

"Very good, Strauth. It's good to know you've been paying attention to something other than just Feya."

"Feya...where is she?"

"I couldn't tell you as I've been waiting for three hours to fish you out of the sea, but if I had to guess, likely the meadow."

Yes. That made sense. "She loves the meadow. And flowers."

A deep chuckle rumbled from Ladisias's chest. "I'd say you sound delusional, but both statements are accurate. However, I do believe there is something she loves more than either of those two things. My catch today will surprise her, I think."

"How did you know I would come? The birds—"

"The birds. The message. All me."

Him? Did that mean Aldeth didn't know? Perhaps Ladisias should have just let him drown.

Strauth pushed himself into a sitting position. Sand clung to every inch of him, as well as the parts of his clothes that didn't hang in shreds. "Your father will kill me. I thought he had sent the message."

Ladisias bellowed and smacked him on the shoulder, making him flinch. "My father has not changed his mind about you in the slightest. I'm afraid that will take a great deal of effort on your part. Admittedly, I wasn't certain of you myself. I wondered if you'd attempt to come ashore once you'd seen how treacherous the current was, but you didn't disappoint me. Your feelings for my sister must run *very* deep to compel you to do something so foolish."

Was that supposed to be a compliment? Regardless, Strauth could hardly argue against his words. It *had* been an incredibly foolish thing to do, and yet, he couldn't bring himself to regret it...at least not now that he hadn't drowned.

"Do you intend to protect me from your father, because I suspect he won't take my showing up well?"

"That depends."

Strauth attempted to brush the wet sand from his trousers, but the effort proved pointless. "Depends on what?"

A wide smirk crossed Ladisias's face. "On your intentions. Why exactly did you come?"

"I should think it obvious, but if you insist I say it, then I came because I love your sister. I can't fathom a life without her in it."

"And?"

Strauth scowled, which only made Ladisias laugh again. He leaned forward and, for whatever reason, felt the need to whisper. "This is the part where you tell me you intend to offer for her hand, because it's the only way I'm allowing you anywhere near her."

"Very well. Should your father *not* kill me at first sight, I intend to ask her to marry me."

Ladisias clapped, and the sound made Strauth's ears ring. "By Virgamor, we should get you cleaned up then. I can't have you proposing to my sister looking like some castaway." He stood and gestured for Strauth to do the same. Lightheadedness made the scenery spin, but the feeling dissipated after a moment.

"There's a stream just a few minutes up the trail," said Ladisias, pointing towards the forest. "You can wash off there. I've even taken the liberty of bringing you some clothes. My mother found you a few things. Figured you'd want to look somewhat presentable."

"Your mother knew I was coming?" Aldeth didn't know, but did Feya? Wouldn't she have come with her brother if she had? The uncertainty made him squirm. Now that he knew Ladisias had sent him the message, he couldn't be sure Feya had forgiven him at all. What if she hadn't?

"Well, I had little choice but to tell her," said Ladisias, starting towards the path. Strauth trotted after him, still a little shaky on his feet. "My mother can see the future, or at least she can occasionally. I learned at a young age that hiding things from her was a pointless endeavor. So, rather than risk her having a vision and telling my father, I told her myself."

"And how did she respond?" Aldeth hated him, but perhaps Feya's mother would give him a chance. The more people he could win over, the less likely Aldeth was to *actually* kill him. Ladisias seemed to trust Strauth—at least enough to get him to Verascene and save him from drowning.

"At first, she didn't believe me," he answered with a chuckle. "I don't know if Feya has made you aware, but I'm rather fond of a good joke now and again. Perhaps too often for my mother's liking."

Feya had mentioned that her brother liked to tease her, and having now met Ladisias properly, he didn't doubt her accusation. The man seemed as carefree and jovial as they came.

"Once she realized I was quite serious," he continued, "she responded as most mothers do when their daughters are about to receive a proposal—with complete and utter merriment."

"She was...happy?" asked Strauth with a slow hesitation that reflected his doubt.

"Delighted." They stopped next to a stream, and Ladisias gave him a friendly push towards the water. "Wash off. I've put a change of clothes just there on that rock. I'll go wait over here until you've finished."

Ladisias left him alone to clean up, and Strauth washed sand out of crevices he hadn't even known existed. The new clothes fit him a bit tight, but they would do and were certainly better than his shredded military uniform.

He walked up the path to where Ladisias leaned against an oak tree, and the man clapped upon taking notice of him. "There we are! That looks much better. I suppose we ought to get the hard part over with. Come with me."

Strauth followed behind Ladisias for what felt like ages. His eagerness and fear only grew when they left the forest and entered a wide clearing. About a dozen cottages with bright red roofs rested in the distance, along with what looked like a forge and several corrals. They followed the path right into the center of the village, and Strauth's lungs seemed incapable of pulling in air.

Any moment now, he might face death a third time.

They approached a cottage, and Strauth's gaze darted to the crescent moon-shaped window above the door. Ladisias didn't bother to knock, and Strauth followed him inside. The smell of freshly baked bread hit him the moment he entered, and had he not spotted Aldeth sitting at the table, the tantalizing aroma might have distracted him.

Aldeth glanced up briefly and then did a double-take, his eyes fixating on Strauth and his face turning as white as linen. The chair screeched across the floor as Aldeth stood, fists clenched. "What is he doing here!"

Ladisias stepped in front of Strauth and held up his hands. "Papa, stay calm. I brought him here."

"I can see that! Why would you bring the man who tried to kill your sister into our home?"

"Because my sister has been depressed since she left him sitting in that barn. Don't pretend you can't see their affection for each other."

Aldeth peeked around Ladisias, and Strauth took a step back, bumping into the door. "I don't care how he feels about her! I won't let him anywhere near Feya. She may not understand, but I'm doing what's best for her, and you've brought this monster right into our midst. Now he knows where we live. You think he won't run back to Delran with the information?"

Strauth could just barely make out Ladisias's scowl. "If he wanted to tell Delran, he would have done so already. He wouldn't have tried to come ashore in a dinky rowboat like an idiot." Ladisias glanced at him over his shoulder. "No offense."

"None taken," muttered Strauth. As if he could when the man was the only thing keeping Aldeth from strangling him.

An annoyed sigh sounded from the other side of the cottage, and Strauth leaned sideways just enough to see Yelene rushing towards them. She pushed past the two men and grabbed him by the arm. "Don't worry about these two. Come with me. You must be starving."

He *was* quite hungry, but at the moment, he was far too afraid of Aldeth to even think about putting something into his stomach. He allowed Yelene to guide him to the table, but hesitated to sit down. "I...that is kind of you, but—"

"Yelene, what are you doing?" Aldeth growled, moving towards them. She stepped in front of him before he could reach Strauth.

"Right now, I'm protecting my future son-in-law from you. Dearest, you need to calm down. Strauth may have once planned to help his brother, but he has also risked his life for our daughter. Whatever is in the past must be laid to rest. We cannot keep going like this."

"Then allow me to finish what I started in Izarden."

Ladisias grabbed his father by the shoulder, holding him back. Yelene pursed her lips and her brow furrowed. "You aren't going to lay a hand on him. Now go calm down, or you won't get any pie later."

Aldeth scowled and swatted his son's hand from his tunic. "Yelene, that man—"

"Saved our Feya from an assassin."

"An assassin he and his brother hired!"

The last thing Strauth wanted was for them to argue. He'd already made a mess of things, and he didn't need another to clean up. "Enough!"

Everyone froze.

"Listen, I know I've been a complete fool. I've made horrendous mistakes, and I wish I could take them back, but I can't change the past. All I can promise is that I will do better—that I will do right by your daughter. I love her with every ounce of my being. She deserves to be happy, and I can't help but believe she could be with me. I don't deserve your trust, and I won't ask for it, but please give me a chance to earn it."

Aldeth folded his arms and glared. "I believe you once said you could never trust magic, so why should I offer you mine?"

Strauth grimaced. He'd spat those words the day he met Aldeth in the Great Hall. It seemed like so long ago and much had changed. How he wished he could take them back.

"I don't blame you for your anger and frustration. If anything, I deserve it. But I will not let that stop me. I couldn't stay in Izarden—and not just because I'd be tried for treason for my actions—but because I don't want a life without her in it. Feya opened my eyes to the truth. She found me when I didn't even know I was lost. If you must kill me, then so be it, but I refuse to just give up on her. My heart will not allow it."

Aldeth muttered something under his breath that sounded like a curse, though whether it was simple disdain or a spell, Strauth couldn't say. Hopefully, not the latter.

Yelene placed a hand on her husband's chest. "Aldeth, please. I've already lost my son. I cannot lose my daughter too."

Aldeth's face softened, and he raked his hands through his hair. He seemed to ponder his wife's words, seconds that felt like hours, before turning to face Strauth. His tone came far less harsh, almost calm. "What exactly are your intentions?"

"To marry Feya, if she'll have me. And I wish to have your blessing."

The man considered him for a moment, and Strauth thought his heart might pound completely out of his chest. "I don't trust you, but I do trust my daughter. If Feya is willing to accept your proposal, then I'll not stop her. You have my permission to offer for my daughter's hand, but I cannot—will not—ever give you my blessing."

Aldeth pulled out of his wife's grasp, and with the bang of the door, left the cottage. Strauth exhaled.

"Well, I suppose that could have gone worse," said Ladisias. "At least you're still alive."

"I have the two of you to thank for that. Speaking on my behalf was likely the only thing that kept me breathing."

Yelene sauntered forward, and to Strauth's astonishment, pulled him into an embrace. "I know he seems difficult, but he will come around. You have earned my trust, Lieutenant, and I look forward to welcoming you into our family."

A lump swelled in his throat as she pulled away. "That means a great deal to me, but you should know, I am no longer a lieutenant. I hope that doesn't devalue my proposal to your daughter."

Yelene chuckled and patted his face. "Not in the slightest. Titles are of little value here, Strauth. The only thing that matters to us is that you and Feya are happy, and I am very hopeful you both shall be."

Strauth's lips lifted. "Thank you."

Ladisias groaned. "I've wasted my entire day on sappy sentiments. Come on, Strauth. I'll take you to my sister so we can be done with this mushiness."

"Good luck, dear," said Yelene, tapping his arm. "I don't believe you'll need it, though. Ladisias, be sure the *three* of you are back for dinner at sunset."

The giddiness with which she said *three* warmed Strauth like someone had shoved the sun down his throat. Yelene had been so accepting of him, and he had felt more affection from her in a matter of minutes than he'd ever physically received from his own mother.

Ladisias guided him along a dirt path out of the village, and Strauth's heart rate increased again. Feya's family seemed convinced she would be glad to see him, but doubt still gripped him.

"Let me talk to her first," said Ladisias. "You stay back and keep quiet."

"Why?" Did Ladisias think his presence would upset her? His stomach rolled.

Ladisias's wide smirk returned. "Because I've spent the entire day helping you—several days, in fact—and I think I deserve a reward for it all. I may as well establish my position as favorite brother and milk the situation for everything that I can. Now, keep quiet and stop when I tell you to."

Strauth nodded. If the man wanted praise for bringing him here, Strauth would be happy to provide it. He owed Ladisias a great debt for giving him a chance.

They entered a clearing dotted with yellow and white flowers, and the moment Strauth's gaze landed on Feya, his breath caught. She faced away from them, sitting on a mat of lush green grass with his black military coat wrapped around her shoulders. The sight sent flutters dancing through his insides. Perhaps she did miss him.

The soft blades muffled the sounds of their footsteps, allowing them to go unnoticed. Ladisias held his hand out to stop Strauth when they were but a few yards away from her.

Feya may not have heard their approach, but Strauth felt certain the thuds beating against his chest would give them away, and part of him hoped they would. But he waited quietly, as Ladisias had instructed, for the woman he loved to turn around.

CHAPTER TWENTY SIX
Love and Magic

Ladisias plopped down on the grass beside Feya, and for several long moments, the two of them sat in silence. She had been enjoying her time alone, though it had done nothing to ease the pain.

"If you've come to pester me, I'm not in much of a mood for it."

"I haven't come to pester you...well, maybe a little. You know I can't help but do it."

Feya plucked several blades of grass and tossed them in front of her. "Is Papa still upset?"

Ladisias snorted, which made Feya's brows draw together. "He's likely more upset now than he was this morning, but don't concern yourself over it. This time it was my doing, not yours." Ladisias moved his arm behind her and leaned closer. "I'm sorry about everything, Feya. I know how difficult the last few days have been. We all care about you and just want you to be happy. I hope you know that."

She did. Even in her frustrations with Papa, she knew he only had her best interests at heart. He just didn't understand, and since she would never see Strauth again, it didn't matter. She should let her anger go. But letting the man she loved go was another thing entirely.

Feya tugged Strauth's coat tighter around her. The air was hot, and the fabric made her sweat, but it was the only thing she had left of him. Even the woody scent that lingered on it filled her mind with memories. Someday the smell would fade, but she hoped those moments with Strauth would remain vivid.

"I do know, and I appreciate your concerns. I couldn't ask for a better family"—she poked him in the side a few times, making him laugh—"pestering and all."

"It's good to see you smile," said Ladisias. "Especially since I need to ask you a very serious question."

What did her smiling have anything to do with a serious question? Feya narrowed her eyes, and a lopsided grin appeared on his lips.

"I need you to be in a good mood when I ask because I suspect you might get mad at me for it, but know that I do nothing without purpose."

"The purpose of driving me crazy, perhaps. Your teasing could serve little else, and that mischievous look of yours tells me that's exactly what this question will be."

He stared at her, and the mirth faded from his expression. "Do you love the lieutenant?"

Her stomach lurched, and heat flooded her cheeks. "Ladisias, this isn't funny. I don't wish to—"

"I need to know whether you love him or not."

"Why? Do you not understand how painful that question is? Yes, Ladisias, I love him! I love him and I will never have the chance to tell him so. That alone is enough to shatter what little remains of my heart. Is that what you wanted to hear?"

His lips lifted, but not in amusement. There was contentment in the way he looked at her. "I'm sorry to have upset you, but I needed to be sure. Also, I thought Strauth might enjoy hearing you say it as well."

Feya's face contorted, and Ladisias, with his mischievous smirk, nodded behind them. She turned, and her mouth dropped. Standing but a few yards away from her was Strauth—her loathsome lieutenant. The man she loved.

Ladisias's bellowing laugh surrounded her as she scrambled to her feet, nearly tripping over her dress. Feya dashed forward, losing the coat in her sprint, and threw herself into Strauth's outstretched arms. He lifted her from the ground and held her tight. She gripped his shirt, afraid this was nothing more than an illusion.

His breath tickled her neck, sending shivers across her skin. "I missed you," he whispered. "I'm so sorry."

Unable to speak, she tightened her hold around his neck. Tears streamed from her eyes. Strauth sat her down and pressed a soft kiss to her forehead. No, this wasn't a dream, and the realization left her so elated the world spun.

"I can't believe you're here." She lifted her chin, and after wiping her eyes free of moisture, gave him a pointed look. "What were you thinking? Do you know how dangerous it is? The waters around Verascene are treacherous." Her covered her mouth, muffling her gasp. "And my father! When he finds out—"

"He already knows," said Strauth, chuckling. He swiped a strand of her hair behind her ear, and she committed the accompanying sensation to memory. "Your brother has kept me safe every step of the way, including when I met with your father."

Feya glanced at Ladisias, whose wide grin remained fully in place. "Just admit it," he said. "I'm your favorite."

She didn't like to make preferences, but right now, he certainly was. Strauth curled his fingers under her chin and brought her gaze back to him. "I'm happy to tell you the whole story, but first, there is something I need to ask you."

He fell to one knee before her, and Feya's heart stopped. "Feya, I have made countless mistakes, and I'm certain they will not be the last, but if you can find it within yourself to forgive me, I would like you to become my wife. Please give me the opportunity to make you as happy as you have made me. I promise to make you laugh and smile as often as I can, to keep you safe and always protect you. You've taught me to feel things I never had before, and I love you more than I ever thought I could love another person. I wish to spend the rest of my life with you, however long your father may allow that to be. Feya, will you marry me?"

She tilted her head and lifted her brows. "Do you promise to read me stories and hold me close? I believe that has always been part of my stipulations. Be sure to look me in the eye when you agree to them."

He chuckled, and the smile that appeared made her heart stutter. "I promise. But you've forgotten one very important stipulation."

Strauth rose and pulled her close. His lips captured hers, and Feya melted against him. He held her nape, and she became lost to him, the sounds of the meadow fading away until all that existed were the two of them. He kissed her more than once or twice, exceeding the terms of their agreement, but she wasn't about to complain.

"You know, I am still sitting here," said Ladisias. "I may have fished your future husband out of the sea, but that doesn't mean I want to watch the two of you maul each other's faces. Probably best you don't do it in front of Papa either."

Feya pulled away from Strauth and glanced over at her brother with a devilish grin, planting her hands on her hips. "You could always go home so you needn't watch."

"And leave you unchaperoned? We've already left you unattended enough as it is and look what happened. If you don't want our father to change his mind and kill him, then I suggest you stick to the proper rules of courtship."

"He's right, you know," said Strauth. "I want to do this the right way. If I'm to earn your father's trust and respect, I must act the perfect gentleman."

Feya pouted. "I suppose you're right, but if I am to endure such torture, then I'd best get one last kiss."

Ladisias groaned, and Feya shifted back into Strauth's arms. She waved one hand in a circular motion, and light expanded from her palm until a shimmering globe encompassed them. In the privacy of her purple bubble, she and Strauth shared several kisses, their love renewed right along with her magic.

"You never answered my question," Strauth whispered before pressing his lips against her neck.

Feya leaned back to look into his steel-blue eyes, for that was how one saw another's truth, as her lieutenant had once taught her. "Yes, I will marry you. I love you, Lieutenant Strauth.

EPILOGUE

The Prodigal Brother Returns

Light chirps sounded through the warm air, a familiar melody for their nightly walks. The sky displayed an ombré of oranges and pinks, and the subtle hint of salt on the breeze made Feya's nose wrinkle. She halted on the path and sucked in a deep breath as pain shot through her abdomen. An arm wrapped around her shoulder and fingers trailed up and down her skin.

The contractions were getting worse.

She held her breath until the pain subsided and her body relaxed.

"Are you certain you wish to keep walking?" asked Strauth.

"Yes. It helps."

"It doesn't look like it helps."

Feya flashed him a scowl, and he held up his hands. "All right, but can we at least walk *towards* the village? I'd prefer your mother be nearby to help. I don't have the slightest clue how to deliver a baby."

"Very well. I suppose I cannot fault you for that."

They turned around, and Feya held onto Strauth's arm as they made a slow pace down the path. "You know, we haven't come up with a name for a girl yet," she said, rubbing a circle on her swollen stomach. They'd chosen Fyord for a boy to honor Strauth's father, but what if they didn't have a boy? They couldn't call their child *baby* forever.

"That's because every time I make a suggestion, you tell me you hate it."

Feya bit her lip. She couldn't deny the accusation. "Well, then come up with better suggestions."

"How about Edelin?" he asked with a smirk.

Feya whacked his shoulder, which only made him laugh.

"Would it not be easier if you came up with one you liked? Seems like it would save me a lot of troub—oww!"

She reminded herself to breathe, but her fingers still dug into her husband's arm. She released a slow breath, and Strauth's brows pinched. "Perhaps I should carry you back to the house? They are growing quite frequent now."

She nodded, but before Strauth could scoop her into his arms, the bush next to the path shook, sending bone chilling swishes echoing through the air. Strauth stepped in front of her, his eyes fixed on the shadows.

A figure emerged from between two boxwood shrubs and brushed the stray leaves from his coat.

"Zeeran?" said Feya, wondering if hallucination was a symptom of childbirth.

Her brother's gaze lingered on Strauth for a moment and then slid to her rounded belly. "You! What did you do to her!"

"Nothing!" said Strauth, pushing her backwards as Zeeran stomped forward. "I mean, I did do that, but it's not—"

"How dare you lay a hand on my sister!" Zeeran grabbed Strauth by the collar and yanked him away from her. Feya focused on the magic flowing through her veins, but another contraction stole her attention. She groaned and stumbled against the tree, digging her fingers into the bark.

Both men appeared at her side with concern-riddled expressions. "Feya, what's wrong?" asked Zeeran, placing a hand on her shoulder.

Strauth swatted her brother's hand away. "She's in labor!"

Blue light surrounded Zeeran's hands, and Strauth stiffened. "It wasn't enough for you to take her prisoner, but this"—he pointed to her stomach—"you had to defile her as well! I'll kill you."

"I suppose you had better get in line behind your father, then. But I don't think your sister will appreciate you murdering her husband."

"Her husband?"

Feya held her stomach and moaned as another contraction paralyzed her with pain. "If you don't stop, I'll kill you both myself," she said through gritted teeth.

Strauth swept his arm under her knees and tucked her against him. "If you must kill me, then at least wait until I've taken care of your sister. I need to get her home."

He didn't wait for Zeeran to respond, but Feya could hear twigs snapping beneath her brother's boots as he followed them back to the village. Strauth pushed open the door and scurried to the back of the cottage. Zeeran pursued them into the bedroom, where Strauth laid her on the bed and placed a soft pillow behind her.

"I'll go get Evree and your mother," said Strauth, brushing her hair from her face and kissing her forehead. "Hang on, love."

She nodded. Having Mama and Evree at her side would certainly help put her racing heart at ease. Mama, at least, had experience giving birth, and Evree had become Feya's best friend during the last two months. Things hadn't been easy after marrying Strauth, as Papa still hated him and had made no effort to hide that fact. Her parents had left Verascene for a time to go in search of her cousin, Eramus, and the brief reprieve had been wonderful for her and the man she loved.

They had returned a few weeks later with both Eramus and Evree, who wed not long after their arrival to the island. Upon their return, Papa had immediately reiterated his disapproval of Strauth, but having Evree as a new companion had given Feya someone to complain to. She'd never realized how nice it would be to have a sister.

"Yes," she muttered. "Please go get them."

He turned to leave, but his eyes landed on Zeeran and he stopped in his tracks.

"It's fine, Strauth. My brother won't hurt me. Please hurry."

She groaned, and the sound seemed to snap him out of his indecision. Strauth disappeared out the door, and Zeeran sat down on the edge of the bed. "Talk to me," she said, trying to focus on her breathing.

"About what?"

"Anything. Distract me. Why did you decide to come home?"

Zeeran shifted and stared at the floor. "I just came to visit, not stay. How long have you...been married?"

"A year, which you would know if you hadn't been away so long."

"And did he force you—"

"Virgamor, Zeeran! No, he did not force me to do anything. Strauth is a good man, and I love him."

His shoulders slouched, and the tension faded from his expression. "It seems I've missed a great deal, then. I can't believe you fell in love with the man holding you hostage."

Feya gave him a pointed look, and Zeeran chuckled. He had never been one to tease her often, but she welcomed it now. She'd missed him—worried about him—for months.

"I'm glad you're here, but I do wish you would consider staying. I don't like the idea of you returning to our uncle."

Another contraction tightened every muscle in her body. Zeeran gave her a moment to move past the wave of pain before he responded. "I don't see things the way you do. I believe our uncle was justified in desiring revenge. Sytal was a murderer. I can't blame Morzaun for putting an end to that man's life."

"And what about mine?" she whispered. "Was he justified in desiring to end mine as well?"

Zeeran's brows pinched. "Yours? What are you talking about?"

Feya shook her head. Of course, her uncle hadn't told him. Zeeran would never remain loyal to Morzaun if he knew about the assassin. Perhaps the truth would convince him to stay. "Our uncle hired an assassin to kill me while I stayed at the palace, Zeeran."

"What? That's not funny. Don't joke about—"

"It isn't a joke! I nearly died twice! If Strauth hadn't been there, I certainly would have."

"You must be mistaken, Feya. Why would Morzaun hire someone to kill you?"

Feya managed a shrug just before another contraction took over. What in Virgamor was taking Strauth so long?

"I'm not mistaken," she said through clenched teeth. "The assassin told me he hired her, and she had Uncle Morzaun's dagger. She said I had something he needed."

Zeeran's face went completely pale. "The dagger?"

"Yes, why?"

Her brother rose from the bed and marched towards the door. "Zeeran!" she shouted after him. "Please don't go."

He stopped and turned to look at her. Regret filled his features, but he offered her a small smile. "There's something I need to take care of, but I'll come back as soon as I have. I think it's time I came home."

Her lip quivered. She didn't want him to leave. Although Zeeran had sided with Morzaun, she still loved him. He'd seemed surprised by what she had revealed. Zeeran may not always agree with Papa, and he may believe their uncle was justified in his actions, but he would never do anything to hurt her. She didn't know why their uncle had sought to end her life, but if he had hired an assassin to kill her, what would stop him from doing the same to Zeeran?

"Please, just stay. I don't want you to get hurt."

Zeeran moved back to her side, but rather than sit down, he wrapped her in a hug. "I promise I'll be back soon. Don't worry about me. You have more important things to focus on."

He pulled away, and Feya wanted to tell him again not to leave, but a sharp jolt tore through her stomach, stealing her voice. When she could finally look up, Zeeran had disappeared.

Strauth appeared at the bedroom door several moments later with Evree and her mother on his heels. The two women bustled about the room, though what exactly they were doing, she didn't know. Strauth held her hand, and Feya squeezed it with all the strength she possessed.

"Zeeran," she said between breaths.

"He wasn't here when I returned. We'll find your brother, but right now you needn't worry about him." He leaned forward and kissed her forehead with the tenderness she'd come to expect from her lieutenant.

She nodded, but something told her Zeeran was gone. Had he left to confront their uncle? Feya tried to push the thought from her mind. In her current state, she didn't have room for such things.

"All right, sweetheart," said Mama. "When the next contraction comes, I need you to push."

Push. She could do that. She could do *this*.

The next few minutes were the longest and shortest of her life. Exhaustion compelled her to rest, but her body convinced her to continue. Only when the wail of her newborn child pierced the air did she finally allow herself a moment to relax. A mixture of relief and happiness flooded over her, and when Mama placed the baby in her arms, Feya became overtaken with sobs of joy.

She looked down at the hairless bundle. Petite ears. Tiny fingers. "And the most adorable little nose. She has her Papa's nose."

Strauth chuckled and leaned forward to get a better look. "Are you saying I have an adorable nose?"

"Of course you do," said Evree, giggling from the corner. "She would not have married a man with an ugly nose."

Certainly not.

Feya offered the tiny bundle to Strauth, who took her with an expression full of emotion. She'd only seen her husband cry once, and Feya had thought she'd prefer to never see him do so again, but watching his eyes fill with tears over the life they had created together changed her mind. Tears of happiness were something to be celebrated, not locked away. The world needed them to counteract those of sorrow and grief.

The sound of boots drew her attention to the door. Eramus appeared first and took his place next to Evree, giving her a kiss on the cheek. Papa remained in the door frame, uncertainty stitched on his face. He and Strauth had never been on agreeable terms, and this was the first time Papa had ever entered their home.

Strauth followed her gaze and swallowed when his eyes landed on the man who had once threatened to kill him. The tangible tension made everyone in the room grow quiet, other than her little girl, who filled the silence with her soft cooing. Her husband rose, cradling the child as if she were the most precious thing he'd ever carried, and approached Papa.

"Would you like to meet your granddaughter?"

Papa's face twisted. "May I?"

"Of course." Strauth smiled, and it warmed her heart more than he could know. He'd tried so hard the last few months to earn her father's trust, and to see them interact without an inkling of disdain meant the world to her.

Strauth passed their little girl to Papa, and he smiled down at her with glossy eyes. "She's beautiful," he whispered.

"Like her mother," said Strauth.

"And with any luck, she will be brave like her father, and hopefully, just as patient with her grandfather as he has been."

Understanding seemed to pass between them. Feya relaxed deeper against her pillow and sighed. As she watched her family gather around Papa to meet her daughter, happiness consumed her soul. For a moment, even if it would not last, her entire world was at peace. Only two people were missing from the scene before her, and her stomach twisted at the reminder of Zeeran's abrupt departure.

Where was Ladisias? Had he seen Zeeran? Gone to look for

him?

Zeeran had promised to return, and that filled her with hope. She wanted him to find the same contentment that she had found. A life spent seeking vengeance would never be as fulfilling as one brimming with love. Despite what her uncle believed, revenge and magic would never make them happy.

Revenge and magic were a combination that would only lead them to destruction.

Find out Strauth's and Feya's little girl's name by reading the FREE extended epilogue here:

https://dl.bookfunnel.com/bye90ribl4

Thank you for reading! If you enjoyed this book, please consider leaving me a review on Amazon!

Want more? Visit my website www.brookejlosee.com for character art, excerpts, and more! You can also sign up for my monthly newsletter to get *The Prisoner of Magic* for absolutely free! Just follow this link:

https://bit.ly/VirgamorMessenger

Titles in this series:

Blood & Magic
Love & Magic
Revenge & Magic
War & Magic

Want more stories from this magical world? Check out
my other books!

The Matchmaker Prince
The Prisoner of Magic
The Witch of Selvenor
The Warlock of Dunivear
Origins of Virgàm
The Seer of Verascene
Shadows of Aknar
Path to Irrilàm
The Sorcerer of Kantinar

Acknowledgments

Writing a book requires a team, and I am ever so fortunate to have the best people by my side to help me every step of the way. A big shout out to all those involved in getting this book on the shelves—to you I owe so much. Thank you!

To my wonderful husband, who not only encourages me to continue, but also assists in making my covers. To my beta readers, Justena White, Michelle Dawn, and Brittany Reeves, whose invaluable feedback helped me continually improve and make this story even stronger. To Jake and Mindy Porter for always providing helpful insight and encouragement. To Kaybree Cowley, my number one fan whose demands for the next chapter keep me going. And to all those who continue to support me on this writing adventure, thank you.

ABOUT THE AUTHOR

Brooke Losee lives in Utah with her husband and three children. She enjoys writing, gardening, rock hounding, and just being a *mom*. Brooke appreciates the small town lifestyle and adventurous landscapes of where she lives, often using her background in Geology to aid in her writing. She has always had a passion for science, history, and of course, all things books.